JULIUS ZEBRA

RUMBLE WITH THE ROMANS!

GARY NORTHFIELD

WALKER
BOOKS

Dedicated to Alex Milway,
for his zealous encouragement.

Special thanks to Lizzie and Jack, the best
editor and designer I could ever wish for.

First published in Great Britain 2015 by Walker Books Ltd
87 Vauxhall Walk, London SE11 5HJ

This edition published 2016

2 4 6 8 10 9 7 5 3

© 2015 Gary Northfield

The right of Gary Northfield to be identified as author and illustrator
of this work has been asserted by him in accordance with the
Copyright, Designs and Patents Act 1988

This book has been typeset in Stempel Schneidler

Printed and bound in Great Britain by Clays Ltd, St Ives plc

British Library Cataloguing in Publication Data:
a catalogue record for this book is available from the British Library

ISBN 978-1-4063-6587-0

www.walker.co.uk

CONTENTS

So, you think you know about

ZEBRAS?

knowledgeable
gnu

Why,
yes I
do!

Our handsome hero, Julius!

Well, you're probably

WRONG!

How very dare you!

What most people think they know about zebras...
Yippee!
Eat grass
Mm ... grass! Lovely grass!
Grassy burp
Burp!
Stupid
Woohoo! Check out my booger!
Tut
Unimpressed warthog
Always getting eaten
Rats! Not again!
CHOMP!

What zebras are REALLY like...
This I gotta see.
Grumpy gnu
Loyal to their family and friends
I love you, Mum!
I love you too, son!
Aw! We have the loveliest herd!
Bit of dust in his eye
Can outrun the fastest lions
Puff!
Pant!
ZOOOOOM!
See ya, loser!
And ... er ... Ok, they do actually eat a lot of grass...
Chew!
BURP!
I knew it.
They are definitely stupid, too!
Such a grump!

But Julius wasn't quite like all zebras.

And, to make things even more interesting, he lived in …

ROMAN TIMES!!

EXCITING, RIGHT?

CHAPTER ONE
LAKE OF DOOM

Life on the dusty, shrubby African plains wasn't all fun and games for Julius (i.e. eating grass all day). Every Wednesday, much to his disgust, his mum would drag him and his (very annoying, stupid) brother, Brutus, to the lake.

Julius HATED the lake …

with a PASSION!

He thought all the animals **STANK!**

And that they were SOOO **BORING!**

Not to mention his fear of being eaten at every turn…

On the other hand, Julius's brother, Brutus, *loved* the lake!

And nothing annoyed Julius more than his big, show-off brother.

So, one week, Julius came up with a nifty plan to try and get out of going. "Look, Mum, I've found this little puddle. It'll do me just fine!" he said.

"No!" scolded his mum. "You'll come to the lake just like everyone else."

"But what about all those crocodiles…"

"You'd have to be very old or stupid for one of *those* to catch you," she said.

"What about those ferocious lions, then?" Julius protested.

"Bah! You're more likely to be hit by a flaming rock from the sky than get caught by one of those lazy beasts!"

"But that's ridiculous," said Julius. "I know plenty of zebras who have been eaten by lions. That has to be the stupidest thing I've ever heard!"

"Now, get to the lake this instant, or a lion with big teeth will be the least of your worries!"

Just as Julius was nursing his bruised bottom, Brutus strutted up to him. "Come on, bruv. The lake is brilliant! Far more exciting than your silly puddle."

And before Julius could do anything about it, Brutus grabbed him by the front hooves and spun him round.

"Can you do amazing, backward somersaults into your puddle like we do at the lake? Let's find out!"

"Nope, thought not! Come on, nincompoop – last one there is a warthog!"

And with that, Brutus pranced off with the rest of the herd.

"Come on, Julius, drink up. It will give you strength!" said his mum.

Julius sniffed the water, then creased up his face.

"If you don't drink up, you won't grow big and strong like your brother Brutus. You'll become a weakling – easy prey for any hyena or lion."

"But it *stinks*!" cried Julius. "What with all those crocodiles and hippos doing their whatnot in it. I don't know how *anyone* can drink this filth." His face twisted into a grimace as he took another sniff.

"Look at Brutus," she said. "Do you see him being afraid?"

Nothing about Brutus surprised Julius. That idiot would lick the dribble from a hippo's mouth if he thought it would impress his friends.

"I don't care," insisted Julius. "I still ain't drinking it. You can keep your pooey water – I'm going home." He turned on his hooves and started heading back up the ridge.

Julius didn't fancy getting another kick up the bum. So, reluctantly, he turned back.

As the rotten aroma of the lake wafted up his nostrils, Julius tried to imagine he was standing at the foot of the most beautiful crystal-clear pool, filled with the purest sparkling water that had trickled down from an ancient glacier high up in the mountains.

He counted to three, then took a big GULP...

It tasted REVOLTING!

No stupid pretending was going to hide how vile THAT was.

"There, that wasn't so bad, was it?" piped up a little voice.

Julius looked down to see a small, fat warthog with a toothy grin beaming up at him.

"Don't worry," continued the warthog. "You soon get used to it."

I've been drinking the stuff for years!

How warthogs annoyed Julius. They always thought they were *so* clever. This was the last straw. Now he'd *really* had enough.

"NO, Julius!" she scolded. "We've only just got here. Stop being such a big baby!"

Bah! thought Julius. *I'm no baby. I'll show them! I'll trot back home on my own and when they all finally turn up, they'll realize I'm* more *than capable of looking after myself.*

So, moving very slowly and quietly, Julius slipped away from the herd. He tiptoed up the hill, crouched behind a big boulder and surveyed the landscape, trying to figure out his next move.

"Where are you off to, then?" squeaked a familiar little voice.

"Leave me alone!" barked Julius, waving the warthog away.

"But there're all sorts of lunatics with big teeth prowling around out here. You should be careful," said the warthog.

"Well, you'd better get back to your friends, then," snapped Julius. "We zebras are pretty capable of outrunning lions and the like, thank you very much. But I'm not sure I fancy *your* chances."

"Don't you underestimate us warthogs," he warned, wagging his hoof. "We're *more* than able to dodge the wild beasts of *these* plains. Why, in fact, I think you'll find the average speed of an adult male warthog…"

Julius was heading back the way he'd come. Or so he thought. He wasn't exactly sure. He'd been distracted by some tasty shrubs when he should've been watching where he was going.

Anyway, it doesn't matter, he thought. *I'm FREE! I can walk wherever I want now!*

"Mr Zebra! Sir! I insist that you come back to the lake. It really is very dangerous out here!" said the little warthog, scampering after him.

Julius spun round. "Go away! Why do you suddenly care about me? If you speak to my mum and my brother, you'll soon find out I'm not worth bothering with."

"Your mother does sound quite insistent..." said the warthog, who was really beginning to worry now. But Julius marched on, defiantly.

Then, out of the blue, a frantic family of gnus thundered past.

They were followed by giraffes and antelopes, barking alarm calls and crying for help.

"You know, perhaps we should go back after all... I don't want Mum and Brutus thinking I've been eaten or something," said Julius, scooting back towards the watering hole.

"But wait!" called the warthog. "It's not safe! There's a lion on the loose!"

But when they jumped over the ridge and reached the lake it was absolutely deserted. No zebras, no antelopes, no animals left at all – nothing but clouds of dust.

Julius ran to the spot where he'd stood earlier with his mum and Brutus. "I don't understand," he gasped, looking at the chaotic mess of footprints in the dirt. It was completely impossible to work out which way everyone had gone.

The warthog gave Julius a gentle nudge. "Um, I think maybe we should leave too…"

"But we have to figure out what's happened!"

"Erm … I'm afraid there's not enough time," said the warthog, staring ahead and slowly backing away from the water's edge.

Peering in the same direction, all Julius could see was the silhouette of a solitary lion emerging from the dust clouds. Nervously, he started to back away too.

"B-but how can one lion cause so much trouble? Surely there were others, too?"

"That is a nomadic lion," said the warthog, knowlingly. "He works alone and is far more wily than your ordinary lion."

From across the water, the scruffy-looking beast narrowed his eyes at Julius and the warthog and, baring his great white pointy teeth, he let out a low, rumbling growl.

Come on! We should totally get out of here!

GRR!

They were about to turn tail when a chilling sound of snarling and barking echoed round the lake – a sound unlike anything Julius had heard before.

The lion was also startled and jumped backwards. Through trees in the distance, a pack of agitated wolves bolted straight for him.

Taking their chance, Julius and the warthog scrambled up the ridge in panic and ran as fast as their legs could carry them.

But as they leapt and landed, the loose red soil collapsed from under their feet and they plummeted down to the bottom of a huge pit.

This really is most peculiar!

"WHAT IDIOT PUT THIS STUPID HOLE HERE?!" screamed Julius, pushing the warthog's hairy bottom off his face.

The warthog brushed himself down. "I have heard stories about these pits and, if I'm right (and I dearly hope I'm not), we could be in quite a nasty pickle."

Julius was just about to ask what a pickle was when another large bundle of fur and bones thumped on top of him.

"'ERE! WHAT'S GOING ON?!" he shouted, desperately trying to heave the big lump off. "WHY DOES EVERY IDIOT HAVE TO LAND ON MY HEAD?"

Realizing who it was, they both frantically scrabbled up the sides of the pit and launched into high-pitched screams: "LION! LION! GET US OUT! GET US OUT!!"

But their wailing couldn't be heard above the savage snapping and barking of the wolves. Then, nearby, a booming voice bellowed from above, "Away, boys, away! I need these creatures ALIVE!"

Julius slumped to the floor of the pit and sighed a deep sigh.

❧ CHAPTER THREE ❧
ON THE ROAD

As Julius quivered at the bottom of the dark hole, listening to the grim voices above, he felt a stream of emotions bubbling up inside him. He was scared and angry, and also very confused.

Number one, he thought. *NEVER call a zebra a 'stripy horse'. Zebras are nothing like horses!*

presents:

A HORSE AND A ZEBRA

A ZEBRA

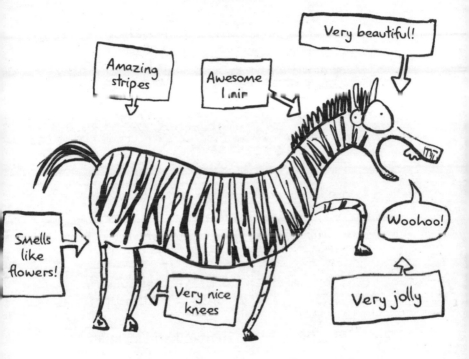

JULIUS SAYS:

LIKE EACH OTHER!

Number two, he puzzled. *What's the story with the bloke with the dead bird on his head?! And why is he so shiny?*

Shiny bowl on head?

Dead bird?

A big stick?

Shiny clothes?

Shiny knees?

But before Julius could demand an explanation, two burly men threw a net over the three animals and hauled them out of the pit on a big pole.

"Throw them into the last box!" barked Dead Bird Hat Man, pointing his stick towards a line of carts in the distance.

His men heaved the bulging, squirming net over to
the caravan and shook the beasts out into the back of
one of the carts like breadcrumbs from a bedsheet.

In a desperate bid to get away from the lion, Julius
and the warthog squished themselves up against the
sides of the box. But, bizarrely, the lion didn't seem
the least bit interested in them and, instead, curled up
on the floor, exhausted.

Poor Julius could not believe his rotten luck. There
he'd been, enjoying his moment of freedom, when
the next thing he knew he was being cooped up with
a lion and a warthog!

"Don't worry, my friend," said the warthog.
"Wherever they're taking us, I'll have plenty of stories
and interesting facts to keep us entertained on the way."

"HE'S STARTING ALREADY!! OH PLEEEEASE!!!
SAVE MEEE!!!"

Let me out!!
You can't leave
me in here!!

But Julius's pleas were ignored by Dead Bird Hat
Man, who simply galloped up to the caravan of carts
and screamed, "Get these beasts moving! If we miss
the boat, you'll ALL be thrown into the arena!"

Julius pulled his head in from the window and sank
to the floor of the cage with a sigh. "I don't know

what's going on any more: boats, arenas, a shiny
bloke with a dead bird stuck to his head? The whole
world's gone bonkers!"

"Well, for a start," said the warthog, helpfully, "the
chap with the bird feathers on his helmet is a Roman
soldier. Possibly a centurion."

Julius looked bemused. "A 'sen-choo-we-oo'?
What's one of them?"

"Well, I'm very glad you asked!" grinned the
warthog. "Now, from what I've heard, these Roman
chaps come from a strange, faraway land and,
basically, they want to take over lots of other strange
lands – mainly by beating everyone up!

"The one in charge wears that feathery hat to
make him look taller than everyone else! And his
big stick shows you he's *boss*. But, watch it – he'll
happily whack you if he doesn't like you."

Julius put his head in his hooves and started to sob.

"By the way," said the warthog. "My name's Cornelius. Very pleased to meet you."

"Julius Zebra," sniffed Julius, extending his hoof for a hoof-shake.

"Lovely to meet you, Debra," said Cornelius.

"Not Debra, ZEBRA!" blubbed Julius.

Cornelius shrugged his shoulders and offered his little hoof to the shabby-looking lion, who was still lying in the middle of the box. "And you, sir?"

"Oh, no worries," said Cornelius. "Keeping yourself to yourself. I understand, old chap."

The cart began bucking and bumping as it trundled

along the rough dirt track and away from the
watering hole.

"But where are these
Romans taking us? What
do they *want* with us?!"
whimpered Julius, holding on
to the sides for dear life.

"Well," said Cornelius. "I'm pretty sure I overheard
something about an arena. So we're probably off to
the circus to watch the Games, which sounds ever so
much fun and very exciting!"

The lion looked up at the mention of the circus and
let out a big "PAH!"

"So, what happens at one of these circuses, then?" asked Julius, confused.

"Oh, all sorts of amazing things!" chirped Cornelius.

JUGGLING MONKEYS!

DOGS RIDING HORSES!

BEARS DANCING WITH OSTRICHES!

"And you know all of this how?" asked Julius, amazed.

"Oh, my brother's friend, who knows a parrot, who's a great chum with an ostrich, whose mum spoke to a gnu, who definitely, no word of a lie, knew a monkey whose uncle Bob was a *juggling* monkey."

The idea of a circus perked Julius up no end. He might be stuck in a manky box off to who-knows-where, but if there were fun and games to be had, then maybe it was something to celebrate!

"Back home, when we zebras need cheering up, there's an ancient song we like to sing. My mother sang it to me, and her mother before her…" Julius cleared his throat. "Everybody, after me … *THE WHEELS ON THE CART GO ROUND AND ROUND…*"

"Bah! Imbeciles!" groaned the lion.

"Ah, come on, grumpy!" snapped Julius, immediately thinking of the next verse: "*THE GRUMPY LION ON THE CART GOES GRUMP, GRUMP, GRUMP!*"

The lion leapt over to Julius and grabbed him by the throat.

"Calm down, grumpy guts," Julius let out a nervous laugh. "It's just a song – no need to get your whiskers in a twist!"

"Listen, this isn't a joke," growled the lion, pushing his nose up to Julius's face. "Your stupid friend may think he knows everything, but he doesn't. There'll be no fun, there'll be no games, there'll be no coming home again. Where we're going will be the end of the road for us."

"What? No juggling monkeys?" snivelled Julius.

The lion just sneered in his face. "Know this, Debra, the only thing guaranteed is that you'll never see your family again." And with that he threw Julius to the floor.

"The name's ZEBRA!" Julius muttered, pulling himself up. "What is the matter with everyone?! Is that so difficult to understand?"

Do I even look like a Debra?

CHAPTER FOUR
ON THE ROAD AGAIN

The sun was beating down hard and the cart had become very hot and stuffy, bumping along the uneven road. Pretty much everyone was green from cart-sickness.

As the day wore on, Julius got thirstier and thirstier. So much so that he even started to crave the stinky water from the lake – and miss his family too.

All I wanted was to do my own thing, but not like this...
he thought. *Am I really off to some mad distant land to see the circus? How long will I be stuck in this smelly box? Will I ever see my brother and my mum again?*

With all these puzzles racing through his mind, he curled up in the corner and closed his eyes.

Maybe I'll wake up in the morning and it will all have been some horrible bad dream. And, with that, Julius dozed off to sleep.

He woke to the noise of chattering outside. It was night-time now. And, poking his head out of the small window, Julius boggled at all the different shapes, sizes and colourful costumes of people walking past. *What's going on? Where ARE we?* he thought.

The caravan did a sharp turn round a rocky corner and Julius's bleary eyes almost popped out of his head as he fixed them on the most amazing sight he'd ever seen...

"Oh, thank goodness…" He breathed a sigh of relief. "We can finally get out of this stupid little box. I really need to stretch my legs!"

But the two men driving the cart let out a great big belly-laugh.

"'Ere, what's so funny?" asked Julius, rubbing his stiff knees.

"If you think they're just going to let you out," growled the lion, who was also awake, "you're more stupid than you look."

"What do you mean?" sobbed Julius.

"We're not even halfway there yet," snarled the lion.

"Not even half … WHAT? IS THIS SOME KIND OF JOKE?!" cried Julius.

"I'm sorry to say, the lion's quite right," piped up Cornelius, stretching his legs, which had seized up in the cramped box. "This is probably Leptis Magna, the main port round these parts. We've got hundreds of miles of sailing before we get to Rome!"

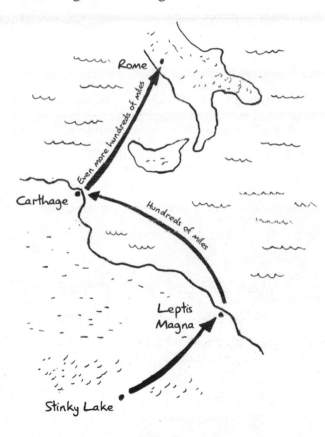

"I just hope your sea legs are better than your land legs," the lion growled. "And you'd better pray to your zebra gods that we don't meet any pirates or get shipwrecked."

"The Romans might be brilliant at beating people up, but they're no sailors," said Cornelius. "I'm certain we'll be fine, though. I saw three crows flying south not five minutes ago, which can only mean good luck lies ahead!"

"Or that three crows were just off on their holidays," said Julius, who wasn't one for silly superstitions.

Cornelius harrumphed loudly and decided to ignore Julius's remark. "Just you see. The flight of a crow has never let me down yet..."

CHAPTER FIVE

I CAME, I SAW, I THREW UP

After their carts had been shoved onto a tiny, ramshackle ship and tossed around by the sea as if it were riding the back of an overexcited hippo, Julius began to think, *This is the worst journey of my life, ever. Fact.*

Peering through the cracks in the walls of his cage, Julius saw that the deck was crammed with crates filled with all sorts of weird animals he had never seen before (and some he had) – all of them groaning with seasickness.

He moaned as the ship rolled on its side, pitching high on a bad-tempered wave. The crates and carts slid along the rain-lashed deck and smashed into its  wall, nearly tipping over the side.

Julius held on for dear life, trying as hard as he might not to fall into the lap of the lion who, he had to admit, looked pretty weak himself.

He noticed Cornelius had gone a queasy shade of green, too.

"SO, HOW ARE THOSE LUCKY CROWS WORKING OUT FOR YOU NOW?" he shouted over the roar of the raging sea and wind.

For once, Cornelius didn't have an answer.

After the storm had gone on for many days –
perhaps weeks – the
exhausted Julius drifted
into a restless sleep. He
dreamed that his brother
Brutus had turned up at
the circus dressed as a
juggling monkey.

Julius had never been so pleased to see his stupid
brother! "Oh, Brutus! You can't believe how much
I've missed you!" he sobbed, giving him a big hug.

"GET OFF!" cried Brutus.

But Julius held on tight. "No, Brutus. Even though
you're a massive idiot,
I'm never letting
you go!"

"Get off me!" Cornelius insisted. "Look outside – we've nearly arrived!"

Julius blushed and let go of the wiry little warthog, rubbed his bleary eyes and peered out to see a man the size of a mountain standing in the sea. "'Ere! Are we sailing to a LAND OF GIANTS?!" Julius blurted out. "That bloke is HUGE!"

"Don't worry, he's not real," squeaked Cornelius enthusiastically.

"Not real?! What *is* he then?"

"Well, I'm glad you asked!" smiled Cornelius, who was ever so excited to dish out his first fact

in two weeks. "That chap out there is a COLOSSUS – a great big statue made of bronze. They're all the fashion these days. Ever since the Colossus of Rhodes became one of the SEVEN WONDERS OF THE WORLD!"

"Cor!" exclaimed Julius. "I wonder what the other six wonders are?"

"No doubt your immense stupidity is *one* of them," growled the lion.

But before Julius could think of a witty reply, there was a great THUD as the ship rolled into port.

"PORTUS AUGUSTI! EVERYBODY OFF!"

CHAPTER SIX

ALL ROADS LEAD TO ROME

"GIDDY-UP!" shouted the drivers as the gangplank clattered onto the quay. And off they scooted, bashing their way through the crowded port.

Julius was amazed at the road – it was so straight and long!

"Aren't the Roman roads fantastic?" remarked Cornelius. "There're no bumpy twists and turns to churn your stomach with *these* chaps."

As they zipped along, Julius barely had time to take in all the grand, shiny buildings lining the road. Instead of the drab scrubland he was so used to, here was a world of magnificent trees and luscious grass.

"After I've watched this stupid circus, I'm going to eat like a king!" said Julius, sticking his tongue out of the cage to lick the grass as it flew by.

The hills and fields were littered with stone trunks, with people standing on them. Julius waved at a few of them, but none waved back.

How rude! he thought.

Dotted everywhere were other stone trees holding up the roofs of houses and even some of the roads.

"The Romans are a clever lot," exclaimed Cornelius. "That road on trees is a river in the air, which carries water to the city. It's called an aqueduct!"

"Wow. An Aqua Duck..." whispered Julius in awe.

"And all *those* stone trees," continued Cornelius, "are columns for holding up heavy buildings!"

Half an hour passed and, as Julius tried to take it all in, suddenly a huge wall with a great doorway loomed up in front of them.

Cooee!

Dead Bird Hat Man dashed ahead on his horse. "Come on! What's the hold-up?" he shouted. "Shift these carts! Emperor Hadrian *himself* is waiting! We can't be late!"

A soldier guarding the archway stood in front of him, blocking his way. "You can't bring these carts through here."

"WHAT?!
WHY NOT?"
screamed
Dead Bird
Hat Man.

I NEED to get these BEASTS to the COLOSSEUM!

"You know the rules, Centurion. No carts through the city after sunrise. Especially on a Saturday. Nothing to stop you *walking* the animals through the street, though..."

Dead Bird Hat Man paused for just a moment. "Ridiculous idea," he barked. Then he turned to his men. "Let's do it! Right, you lot! Grab these animals – COME ON! CHOP CHOP!"

"STOP YER MOANING! GET THEM ANIMALS OUT OF THE CARTS. I WILL NOT BE LATE FOR THE EMPEROR!"

As Julius was hustled through the crowds of Rome – on the shoulders of a hairy brute in a toga – it really dawned on him how far from home he was. The watering hole seemed like a long-distant dream.

"'Ere, Cornelius," he called out. "Are you sure this circus is going to be fun? Some of the things that lion was saying don't exactly make it sound that way."

"Trust me!" Cornelius shouted back. "That juggling monkey is a legend round our parts!"

Julius turned to the lion, who was being carried rather tentatively by a petrified cart-driver. "See, lion, you're talking COBBLERS! How can a jolly circus *not* be fun, eh? You need to *lighten up*!"

"No, Debra, I will NOT lighten up!" roared the lion, before sinking his teeth into the driver carrying him.

The cart-driver dropped the lion like a hot potato and clutched his sore bottom.

And with that, the lion disappeared into the panicking crowd.

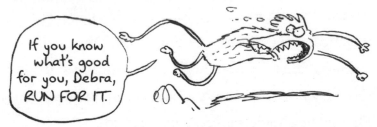

"STOP THAT LION!" screamed Dead Bird Hat
Man. But the beast was long gone.

Over the hubbub of the crowded streets, a huge
roar went up and what sounded like the noise of two
hundred elephants parping.

"Ooh! That's exciting!" said Cornelius. "That'll be
the circus – we must be getting nearer!"

"Forget that!" said Julius, who was really starting
to worry now. "What was that lion going on about?
Maybe we should make a run for it, too…"

Julius, will you forget about that grumpy lion!

Everything is going to be just fine!

"Listen," whispered Cornelius, getting all serious. "I've heard about certain, shall we say *unpleasant*, things that go on in Rome, but they only involve lions and other nasty beasties. *We'll* be all right."

Julius wasn't convinced. That lion seemed to know something the rest of them didn't. But before he could say anything, a jaw-dropping vision towered up in front of him and took his breath away. "Wow," he whispered.

Julius shuddered as the ginormous building bellowed with the noise of ten thousand people. The surrounding streets were crammed with men and women dancing and singing and children walloping each other playfully with wooden sticks. *What on earth are they doing that for?* Julius wondered.

He hadn't liked the crowds at the lake back home, and this seemed ten times worse. As they pushed their way through the swarming throng of people, Julius felt as if he might drown.

"Cheer up, Julius!" shouted Cornelius, spotting his young companion frowning. "Listen to that crowd! Imagine how brilliant the circus will be!"

Julius tried his best to get into the spirit of things: "Yeah, you're right, of course! Bring on the juggling monkeys! Woohoo!" But his bravado quickly evaporated when he realized they were being taken right past the Colosseum! "HEY! WHERE ARE YOU GOING? THE CIRCUS IS BACK THERE!"

"You lot have a *special* entrance into the arena. You're gonna LOVE IT!" the cart-driver said, sniggering.

It was at this moment that Julius hit a cold wall of reality. His stomach churned as if he had swallowed a hundred butterflies. *We're not watching the circus,* he thought… *We're going to be IN the circus!*

"TO THE TUNNEL!" commanded Dead Bird Hat Man.

Julius gulped as he was lugged towards a big buiding round the other side of the main amphitheatre.

"This way!" said the centurion, charging down a dark passageway.

Julius, now panicking about his big moment in the spotlight, spied a group of men idly sitting on the steps, watching the goings-on. "'ERE! DO ANY OF YOU WEIRDOS KNOW HOW TO JUGGLE?!"

"Now why did you go and say that?" asked Cornelius. "You've made them awfully grumpy."

"Aren't they the juggling monkeys? They look like a bunch of hairy gorillas. I don't think they heard me," said Julius. **"I SAID, 'ARE YOU THE JUGGLING MONKEYS?'"**

This greatly enraged the huge hairy men and they stood up and started waving their big swords and sticks, shouting out the most dreadful insults Julius had ever heard.

"Hey! One of them just said I had the face of a goat's bottom! What an outrage!"

"I think you should probably stop talking to them now," said Cornelius nervously.

"I was only asking them a simple question!" snapped Julius. "Ah, well. It's not as if we're ever going to see them again, right?"

At these words, Cornelius went very quiet. The coarse little hairs on his back bristled. It had finally dawned on him that they were in real danger.

As they raced through the tunnel, Julius was struck by a VERY familiar smell. The smell of stinky animals and poo – not unlike that of the lake. He *even* heard the unmistakable, muffled roar of a leopard.

Up ahead, through the gloom, were some doors made of iron bars. In the dim light, Julius could see skulking shadowy figures pacing to and fro behind them.

What's going on here, then? What's in these rooms? he thought. More and more curious, he leaned forward, squinting through the bars into the pungent murkiness.

"ZEBRA!!" a cry went out.

Suddenly all the cells roared and their doors shook as dozens of starved lions, leopards, cheetahs and tigers screamed in unison, "ZEBRA! ZEBRA! ZEBRA! ZEBRA!"

"Well, at least they managed to get your name right," muttered Cornelius.

"Listen, clever clogs," Julius whispered back. "I don't know about you, but that lion was right, we have *got* to get out—"

But before he could finish his sentence, the centurion butted in, "Get this lot over to the cell at the back. I'll eat well tonight – the quaestor has paid handsomely for these beasts, not least because we have a rare stripy horse!"

Julius and Cornelius, along with a giraffe and an antelope, were unceremoniously chucked into a mangy, stinky cell, well away from the bawling predators.

"Cor, blimey. Thank goodness for that!" said Julius, wiping the sweat from his brow. "I thought I was a goner then. Wait, none of you lot has big, sharp teeth do you?"

"AAIIEEE!! A CROCODILE! RUN FOR YOUR LIVES!"

They all scrambled to the door, shaking and pulling at the bars in a desperate attempt to break free.

"Wait! Wait!" said the crocodile meekly. "I'm a vegetarian! I promise I won't eat any of you."

"A vegetarian *crocodile*?" spluttered Julius. "And you expect us to believe that, do you?"

"Oh, I fully understand your distrust, but I assure you I am. Back home in my river, I used to make friends with all the other animals who came along to drink. I couldn't bring myself to eat them, they all seemed so lovely!"

"She's right, you know, Mr Stripy Horse," squeaked a tiny voice. "I ain't never seen her eat nothing other than straw and leaves."

Julius squinted into the darkness. "Who said that? Is there somebody invisible in here?"

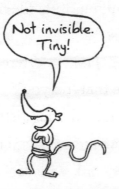

Julius looked at the mouse very curiously. "Are you taking part in the circus, too?" he asked.

"Ooh, no," said the little mouse. "I LIVE HERE!"

"Wait a minute," said Julius, backing away. "Why are you wearing a little nappy? You don't have bottom problems, do you?"

"Ha ha! This isn't a nappy, sir. This is my Subligaria – like what the gladiators wear. I'm Pliny, and when I grow up, I'm going to be one!"

"*Glad-he-ate-her*? Why is everyone so obsessed with eating each other round here?" sighed Julius.

"I'm not," said the crocodile.

"Oh yeah," said Julius, "apart from the weird crocodile."

"I think you'll find our little friend said *gladiator*," explained Cornelius.

"*Gladiator*?" gasped Julius, in exasperation. "What's one of *them*?"

"Gladiators are ferocious fighters who normally battle to the death in an arena – not unlike the one above us. I've heard dark whispers about their exploits … we'd better pray we're kept well away from them."

The crocodile suddenly leapt up and started skipping about like a horse. "Forget gladiators!" she cried. "It's chariot racing I'm excited about! I was lucky enough to

catch sight of a race on my way here. I hope we get to speed around on one of those things!"

"That does sound like much more fun. My name's Cornelius, by the way," said Cornelius. "Very pleased to meet you!" He extended his little hoof and shook paws with the crocodile.

"Lucia," said the crocodile.

"And you…?" Cornelius asked, turning to the others.

"And I'm Julius Zebra!" announced Julius.

"Lovely to meet you, Barbara!" said Pliny.

"You must be a rare breed of horse," said Rufus. "Do you get spotty ones, too?"

"It's ZEBRA!" cried Julius. "And I'm not a flipping horse, either! Have you lot really never seen a zebra before?"

Everyone just shook their heads and shrugged their shoulders. Julius couldn't believe that no one had heard of a zebra – where he came from there were hundreds.

Just at that moment, the cell door was flung open and a scraggy bundle was thrown to the middle of the floor. "Stick him in there. The rascal can go up in the first batch!"

The bundle stood up and launched itself at the iron bars with a ferocious roar. As it fell back to the floor, Julius immediately recognized who it was. "Oh, hello! I wasn't expecting to see you again," he chirped.

"Hello, Milus!" squeaked Pliny. "Come back for more, then?"

"Wait a minute! *Milus?!* You *know* him?" blurted Julius.

"Of course," said Pliny. "I'd recognize that ugly face anywhere! Milus taught me everything I know. This dude has *all* the skills it takes to be a gladiator! He evaded the sword of the Venatores three times before making his escape. I didn't expect to see him back again."

Julius was puzzling over why everyone kept banging on about gladiators, when a cacophony of horns blasted from above, rattling the ceiling.

There was a great roar as ten thousand people cheered and stamped, shaking the walls of their dungeon and sending great lumps of plaster and dust falling on everyone's heads.

"'Ere! It's them blooming elephants again! Has the circus started?" Julius's stomach burbled with nerves. "Can someone *please* teach me to juggle? I've never done it before."

The whole room went silent.

All except for Felix who stood up and walked to the back of the dungeon. "Cor!" he said, bending down. "Look at this weird rock…"

Julius went over to have a look.

"I love rocks, me," proclaimed Felix. "I have quite a collection at home."

Julius picked it up and showed it to Milus. "Come on, grumpy. Look at this funny rock. This should cheer you up!"

"You really are a blithering imbecile, aren't you, Debra!" growled the lion, stepping out of the shadows.

"It's *Zebra!*" said Julius. "*ZEBRA!* When is anyone actually going to get my name right round here?"

"Listen, *zebra*, no one cares about your stupid rock. No one cares about your stupid name. Or *any* of our names. In five minutes we're going to be dog food.

No one will even remember that there ever was a
zebra or a lion or a crocodile or *any of us* sitting here.
We'll be gone – and in ten minutes another bunch of
animals will turn up and get killed, and it'll just keep
happening again and again, *ad infinitum*." The lion
threw Julius onto the floor.

"ALL RIGHT!" shouted Julius. "I GET IT!" He
dusted himself down with his hooves. "We're
all going to die and *no one* will remember us. I
understand! HAPPY NOW?" he sobbed.

I'll remember you,
Barbara.

"Thank you, Pliny," sniffed Julius. "But the name is
Zebra, not Barbara." And he moped off to sit down.

"That's what I said! Cor, touchy, ain't 'e?"

Suddenly, the cell door swung open and a huge
barrel of a man stood in the doorway. "RIGHT, YOU
LOT! YOU'RE ON!" He cracked a whip. "AND THAT
MEANS YOU, TOO, BARBARA!"

CHAPTER EIGHT
VENATIO!

The animals were hustled out of their cell into the murky, stinky corridor, where more scruffy-looking barbarians cracked the air with their whips.

Little Pliny the mouse ran out to give them a big wave goodbye. "GOOD LUCK! YOU SHOW THEM ROTTERS WHO'S BOSS!" he shouted.

Soon they found themselves corralled into a tiny cage – so tiny they barely all squeezed in.

Slamming the door of the cage shut, the Dungeon Master shouted, "Shut yer moaning! All of ya! You'll be out in the lovely fresh air any minute now.

"These people have worked hard all week, so let's give them a show to remember, eh?"

With the handle of his whip, he rapped the side of the cage twice. There was an almighty creaking, groaning sound and slowly it began lifting off the floor, bumping and scraping against the stone walls.

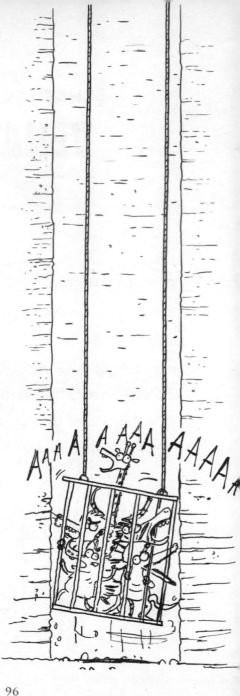

The cage came to a shuddering halt. Everyone was too frightened to say a word.

A trapdoor was opened above them and Julius shivered as a gust of icy air pierced through the bars. They were met with a blinding light, a bamboozling chorus of horns and another almighty roar from the crowd.

Then the cage door swung open.

"COME ON, BARBARA! RUN FOR YOUR LIFE!!"

"Wait!" shouted Julius. But it was too late – everybody had bolted into the unknown.

Bewildered by the dazzling sun, Julius was barged and bumped from left, right and behind. He could just make out shapes rushing about in a panic.

Voices echoed all around him.

"RUN FOR YOUR LIVES!"

"LOOK OUT!"

"MUMMY!"

Then something whizzed past his ears.

"BARBARA! WATCH OUT!" cried Lucia as she dived forwards and skidded in the dirt.

"Oi! Who's firing pointy sticks at us?" screamed Julius.

Another arrow thudded into the ground, inches from his hooves.

He looked up to find a giant shadow
looming over him.

"Ooh!" it said. "A stripy
horse! You'll make a
lovely rug. My wife *will*
be pleased!"And,
brandishing a massive,
pointy club,
it cried, "Say
goodnight,
horsey!"

Only Julius's speedy zebra guile saved him as he nimbly jumped out of the way.

Seconds later, Julius spotted Cornelius running off into the distance being chased by a man with a big, shiny stick. "CORNELIUS!! THE LION WAS RIGHT! THIS ISN'T A JOLLY CIRCUS!!"

One thing is certain, Julius thought. *We have to get out of here and we have to get out FAST!*

But before he could work out how, just in time he spied the same dark shadow falling in front of him.

The big man was getting a bit grumpy now. "Stop leaping out of the way, stupid horse. I want your lovely, stripy hide!" And he struck at Julius again.

"Wait," said a voice. "This one is mine!"

The man lowered his club and stepped away. "Yes, of course, Victorius. The stripy one is all yours."

Now a short, stocky, heavily armoured man stood in front of Julius. His face was hidden behind a visored metal helmet, and he was holding a big, sharp, shiny stick. He pressed Julius against the arena wall.

You're the horse who called us all monkeys.

"Now, look," Julius stammered nervously. "First, I'm not a horse, I'm a zebra. Nothing like a horse. At all. Secondly, I was promised juggling monkeys and I LOVE juggling monkeys, so I don't know why you're so upset, because I was paying you a COMPLIMENT!"

Victorius leaned forward. "You talk too much, horse." And he smashed his sword into the stone wall next to Julius's head.

As Julius scampered away, he spotted something glinting in the sand. He squinted, realizing immediately what it was – A SHINY STICK!

One of those nasty boneheads must've dropped it, he thought, dashing to pick it up. *What luck!* He held it up to have a good look. *Now, how do I use this flipping thing?*

He didn't have to wait long to find out!

"Ha ha!" laughed Victorius. "See how the beast wields a sword. He thinks he's people!"

Victorius held aloft his own sword for a final thrust. "What a curious creature you *were*, horse."

But Julius pulled himself up. "When will you people *listen*? I'M NOT A HORSE…"

ZEBRA!

ZEBRA!

ZEBRA!

Victorius lay on the floor, dazed. He looked at the big new dent in his shield. "You … you HIT ME!" he stammered. "You, a simple animal, ACTUALLY hit me!"

Julius stood looking at his pointy stick, not really knowing what had just happened. "I-I'm really sorry," he whimpered. "I don't know what came over me… Please don't kill me!"

Meanwhile, all around the arena the audience were on their feet, chanting, "Zebra!"

ZEBRA!

ZEBRA!

ZEBRA!

Even the other gladiators had stopped chasing the rest of the animals. No one had ever seen anything quite like it before: an animal fighting back against a gladiator *with a sword*.

Even the Emperor Hadrian, in his gold-and-marble box seat, had woken from his slumber wondering what all the hoo-hah was about.

?

Sigh. Right in the middle of a good dream.

"No animal bests ME!" screamed Victorius.

"You've had your fun, beast. Made a little name for yourself for five minutes."

A huge roar of "BOO" went up around the arena. The whole audience were still on their feet, waving white hankies and shouting angrily at the gladiator.

Ignoring them, Victorius raised his weapon, ready for the final blow. But the crowd went into a frenzy!

The women in the higher seats wailed and cried; rocks were thrown, as well as food.

Some began shouting at Emperor Hadrian, taunting him for such a despicable show!

Not wishing to have trouble on his hands, Hadrian finally stood up.

A great hush fell over the crowd as the Emperor raised his hand.

"Citizens of Rome!" he cried. "What we have witnessed today is a show of bravery that cannot be ignored!"

The crowd rose to their feet and exploded into cheers.

"This poor creature has unwittingly shown us the true path of our glorious Roman Empire. Fate decrees that we must STAND UP against the odds!"

Down in the arena, an exhausted Cornelius ran up to his flummoxed friend. "Huff! Good work, Julius! Phew! You've brought the Colosseum to a standstill, saving all our skins! You've even got the Emperor worried – you nearly started a riot back there!"

But I don't understand...

All I did was fight back. I would've been someone's fancy carpet if I hadn't.

The warthog looked Julius right in the eye. "You know, when I first met you, I thought you were a complete loser, an idiot. Rarely had I met such a dunce."

"Yeah, all right!" blurted Julius. "Don't get carried away."

"But," continued Cornelius, "I was wrong about you. You've got a lot of guts for a funny little horse. And I think your heroics have done you quite the favour."

Julius was touched. He'd never been called heroic before. Bravery was normally left up to his mum or his brother, while he stayed hidden at the back.

Up in the gold-and-marble box seat, the Emperor Hadrian hadn't quite finished. "It is customary in these situations to grant freedom to those the audience take pity on…" he said, looking directly at Julius.

Julius let out a whoop of appreciation.

"But," continued Hadrian, "I see a different path before you. A path of glory. A path showered in fame and riches. A path such as no other zebra has ever walked upon!"

"Thirty days hence is my birthday. A birthday on which the whole of Rome will celebrate our gladiatorial champions," Hadrian bellowed.

"Gladiators from all over the Empire will gather here, in this, the greatest amphitheatre ever built, and do battle till only ONE remains. And that champion of champions will WIN HIS FREEDOM!"

Julius gulped. *Where is he going with this?* he thought.

"And YOU, zebra," cried Hadrian, pointing directly at Julius, "the new People's Champion, will be there fighting for your freedom, too! Fame and wealth you have never dreamed of could be all yours!"

"WHAT!??!" screamed Julius. "That's not a path to fame and glory – that's a path to me getting my head lopped off. I DON'T STAND A CHANCE!!" Julius started sobbing into his hooves.

The sympathetic crowd started booing again and throwing food towards the Emperor. No one upset THEIR champion!

The Emperor waved his arms to calm the people.
"OK! OK!" he said. "Then you shall have the best
training Rome can offer – alongside heroes and
champions – at our world-famous Gladiator School
… Ludus Magnus!"

A teary-faced Julius peeked out from behind his
hooves. "I-I guess that makes up for it a little bit …
sniff…"

"Um…" said Cornelius. "Don't forget you called all
those gladiators *hairy gorillas*…"

"Oh, yeah. So I did." And he began sobbing
quietly into his hooves again.

At that moment, the Dungeon Master entered the arena and grabbed Julius. "Right, come with me, Barbara. I'll escort you to your new home."

"Good luck, Julius!" called out Cornelius, waving him goodbye. "You'll be a brilliant champion!"

This isn't right. I can't leave my friends behind, Julius thought. *After everything we've been through!*

He pulled away from the Dungeon Master and ran up to the imperial box. "WAIT, Mr Hadrian! Sir!" Julius shouted. "Can I bring my friends, too? They'd make great gladiators!"

Hadrian raised his left eyebrow. "What, even the lion?"

"Well, maybe not the lion…"

"OK, the lion, too!" stammered Julius.

"Of course!" Hadrian said and waved them away.

In truth, Hadrian saw no harm in sending Julius and the other animals for gladiatorial training. As far as he was concerned, he was only delaying their inevitable grisly deaths by a few weeks, while at the same time shutting up his disgruntled citizens. It was win-win.

Victorius was OUTRAGED! He threw his helmet to the sand-covered floor like a spoilt child. "For many years I have trained to be a gladiator. It is an honourable profession. These wretched creatures would only serve to humiliate such a noble calling!"

"Hush, Victorius. If you fear the flailings of a whimpering zebra, perhaps you ought to seek a safer, nobler art, like flower-arranging?" And with that, the Emperor turned his back on the arena and retired to his palace.

"WHAT'S WITH ALL THE WILD ANIMALS?! GET THEM OUT OF HERE!"

"Uh-oh," said Cornelius. "He must be the Lanista."

"The *who*?" asked Julius.

"The *Lanista*, the boss. He owns this place and all the gladiators. I'm guessing no one's told him about your shenanigans yesterday."

"I GO AWAY FOR TWO DAYS AND THE PLACE IS OVERRUN WITH VERMIN!"

The Dungeon Master lumbered over to the Lanista.

"WHAT?! Does he not have a zoo to keep his playthings in? Am I not busy enough with the Birthday Games without having to babysit his PETS?"

Julius decided he'd be helpful and explain the situation. "What it is, right," said Julius, striding up to Septimus, "yesterday I won us all a chance to fight in Hadrian's big birthday bash!"

Septimus looked Julius up and down. "IF THIS RIDICULOUS-LOOKING DONKEY DOESN'T GET OUT OF MY SIGHT, I WILL PERSONALLY KICK HIM FROM HERE TO THE FORESTS OF GERMANIA!"

"Well, that's just rude, " said Julius as he skulked away. "I was only trying to help…"

The Dungeon Master tried to calm Septimus down.

It's not for long. Hadrian just wants you to train them till his Birthday Games.

"WHAT?! *TRAIN?!!* Hadrian has finally lost his mind. Gallivanting around his Empire, doing Jupiter-knows-what, then turning up and seemingly knowing MY business better than I do!"

Septimus felt a little tap on his back. He spun round, but no one was there. Then he heard a little cough.

"Hello! I'm down here," squeaked a voice.

"Um, just a quickie," said Cornelius, producing a big pair of flannel pants from behind his back. "These nappies ... do we *all* have to wear them? It's just that this warm weather really does give me the most awful chafing..."

Septimus stomped over to Felix and Rufus, who were having a little scrap with wooden swords. He grabbed the weapons out of their hooves and threw them into a nearby chest. "STOP TOUCHING THE GLADIATOR EQUIPMENT! IT'S NOT FOR YOU! DO YOU UNDERSTAND?"

Julius was now twirling a big trident.

Septimus strode over to him and kicked him hard up the bottom. "AND THAT MEANS YOU, TOO, DONKEY!"

"Careful!" blurted Julius. "That thing is pointy. You nearly had my eye out!"

Septimus had heard enough.

Once again the Dungeon Master sidled up to Septimus, who was red with fury, and whispered in his ear, "Hadrian is paying you 20,000 sestertii for every animal you keep alive until the Birthday Games begin…"

"Twenty thousand sesterstii?" beamed Septimus, rubbing his hands together gleeflully. "Well, why didn't you say so before? That would keep me in aromatic bath oils for YEARS!"

"QUICKLY! QUICKLY!" he barked.

He began pacing in front of them, looking each one
up and down and, every now and then, *right* in the eye.

"So…" he said. "You all want to be gladiators, eh?"

Julius put up his hoof. "Um, I don't."

Septimus spun round on his heels. "Oh, you don't…?"

"No. In fact, I'd like to go home, please."

"OH! You'd like to go *home*, would you?"

Julius nodded his head.

"And would anyone else like to go home too, hmm?"

"Well, congratulations!" Septimus shouted joyfully. "You're all in LUCK!"

The animals looked at one another, very confused.

Septimus continued. "This magnificent school – where you will learn the noble arts of combat and DEATH – is already your home."

Julius put up his hoof again. "So, let me get this right, we can't *actually* go home to our *real* homes?"

Septimus leaned right into Julius's face. "NO!" he bellowed. "YOU WILL LIVE HERE AND YOU WILL DIE HERE. THERE WILL BE NO ESCAPE!" Septimus straightened up and walked back to the centre of the arena. "And if anyone is caught escaping they will be executed immediately."

Felix the antelope put up a hoof. "In that case, may I have a shelf for my rock collection?"

"Rock collection?" spluttered Septimus.

"Well, obviously I haven't brought my collection with me, but I'm often picking up interesting rocks and stones and they always look very nice sitting on a little shelf."

"Now, listen to me, you useless lot," Septimus shouted, wagging his finger at them. "Being a gladiator is a TOUGH business. Your whole life is concerned with FIGHTING and trying not to be KILLED – and that takes a lot of SKILL." He paused for a moment, looking at them very sternly. "This is no place to make friends, either. One day you will most likely face one another and have to fight to the DEATH!"

Felix turned to Julius. "I promise I won't kill you," he whispered.

"I promise I won't kill you, either," Julius whispered back.

"Pinky swear?"

"Pinky swear."

A large, muscular, bearded man entered the arena and began planting big, long poles into the ground. Meanwhile, Septimus strolled over to the chest full of wooden swords and started lobbing them at the animals.

"Take these," he commanded. "Grab a shield from the other chest behind you, and then each of you stand in front of a pole! COME ON! HOP TO IT!!"

"Now!" boomed Septimus. "These poles represent your ENEMY!"

"What? We're only fighting big sticks? That's a relief," said Julius. "I thought we would be up against actual gladiators. This is going to be a breeze!"

"No, you fool!" blasted Septimus. "These are PRETEND gladiators!"

"*Pretend*?" Julius was puzzled. "But they don't even have any arms or legs! Call this a gladiator school? You don't even know how to make a *pretend* gladiator!"

WILL YOU JUST SHUT UP AND LISTEN!!

"I'll have you know that practising with a pole has helped train Rome's glorious army and gladiators for centuries!" thundered Septimus. "We have conquered the ENTIRE known world thanks to the principle of pole training. If it's good enough for ROME, then it should be good enough for YOU!"

Felix raised a hoof to speak. "How about if we paint faces on them? That might make it a bit easier to pretend they're people."

"Look, over here!" shouted Cornelius. "We could use this pot of paint they're whitewashing the walls with!"

"NO! NO! THERE'LL BE NO FACES ON MY FIGHTING POLES!" Septimus wrested away the paint pot and brushes and threw them out of the arena.

He'd finally had enough. "OUT!!" he raged. "Get out, the lot of you! I don't care what Hadrian says – I'm not training a bunch of nincompoops!!"

Suddenly, there was the clacking sound of wood whacking against wood, punctuated by low growls and rasping grunts. Everyone stopped in their tracks and turned round to see where it was coming from.

"MILUS!" gasped Julius.

"Well, well," said Septimus, clapping his hands with glee. "One of the circus freaks seems to know what he's doing!" He strode up to Milus and put his arm round him. "Now, perhaps you wouldn't mind explaining to your friends the importance of the pole training, too!"

Milus grabbed Septimus by the toga and pulled him right up to his face. "They are NOT my friends."

"Now, wait a minute!" said Cornelius, storming up to Milus. "NOT YOUR FRIENDS? If it weren't for Julius, you'd be an archer's pincushion, or have you forgotten already?"

"I do not work with zebras," growled Milus, sitting down on the arena steps. He glanced at the other animals. "And I especially do not work with antelopes."

"Well, how rude," said Felix. "Maybe I don't want to work with a stupid lion, either!"

"Look," pleaded Julius, "NONE of us is pleased to be here! Do you think I'm happy being a thousand miles away from home? Well, I'm not." He glared at Milus. "If we're going to have any chance of getting out of here alive, we should stick together.

Which means you might have to start thinking a bit more like a zebra. As my mum told me just before half the herd was eaten by crocodiles, 'We must stick together, or divided we fall!'"

"Pah!" spat Milus, staring deep into Julius's eyes. "And how well did being a zebra work out for you? The last I saw, you ran off like a big coward and your herd abandoned you. Some plan!"

Julius stomped off. He knew that Milus was right, but he didn't want to let on.

Just then, little Pliny the mouse dashed into the arena. "All right, gang! I heard you all survived. Good work! I knew you'd have it in ya!"

"Zebra, Barbara, Bob, who cares? You're all going to be GLADIATORS! I am WELL jels! You've made some enemies, though. Old Victorius ain't none too pleased at being beaten by a horse." Pliny swaggered over to Milus. "So what's the plan, then, boss? You going to give this lot some extra training to get them buffed up for the party?"

"Come on, Mr Milus!" squeaked Pliny. "You could teach 'em all your fancy tricks, just like you did me! It'll help you get away from this place. Many hooves make light work and all that." With that, he jumped onto Milus's scraggy mane and gave him a noogie. "I can help as well! I know lots of things. All I do all day is watch the fighting."

"OK," Milus sighed under his breath. "But when we get out of here, I never want to see any of you again. And if we do meet, I'm going to eat you, just like I would eat any other zebra or crocodile. Deal?"

Julius let out a nervous gulp. "Deal."

ALL ZEBRAS ANTELOPES ARE IDIOTS SIGNED EVERYONE!!
Debra FELIX LOVES SEPTIMUS.!! XXX XX X
THIS IS THE TRAINING SCROLL OF JULIUS ZEBRA
DEBRA
ANYONE FOUND NICKING IT WILL GET A KICK UP THE BUM!
I'M NOT EVEN JOKING!
B_RP

My first day of training started with me taking the famous GLADIATOR'S OATH, pledging my life to the Familia Gladiatoria - the Gladiator Family!

I will endure being buried, chained, beaten and killed by the sword!

Wait ... what?!

I'm not sure how keen any of us were on taking this pledge seriously. Cornelius, Felix and I had our hooves crossed behind our backs, which meant we didn't mean it.
But don't tell Septimus!!

My first actual lesson was all about the
Ancient Art of Poking. This is when you
position yourself side-on to your enemy,
holding your shield at chest height, and
then POKE with your sword! Simple!
Cornelius and I took this VERY SERIOUSLY.

Septimus told us that poking is the most effective and safest technique for attacking your enemy. It's been used by Roman soldiers for hundreds of years. He also said what you DON'T want to do is wave your sword around, slashing the air, because this leaves you WIDE open to your enemy's attack.

The next big thing we learned about fighting is NEVER take your eyes off your opponent. EVER.

Cornelius, Rufus and I are really getting stuck into our training. We're desperate for a chance to win our freedom, and nothing is going to stand in our way!

We also have loads of after-school tuition from Milus and little Pliny, who are teaching us to use our natural animal skills and attributes alongside the ancient techniques. (Me - speed and agility; Cornelius - brains and speed; Rufus - very long limbs).

Felix and Lucia never really show any
interest in the art of hand-to-hand combat.
Felix is more interested in his rocks.

And Lucia, well, who knows what she gets up to.
She never seems to be at training, that's all I know.

Come to think of it, Rufus isn't always
at training, either.

We are also causing a bit of a stir among the proper gladiators in the school. Victorius, my rotten opponent in the amphitheatre, is the ringleader, of course! It turns out that none of the ugly brutes took kindly to my calling them "juggling monkeys" - nor to their big leader, Victorius, being beaten by a "stupid horse". They are dead set on making all our lives a misery!

They trip us up, push us into puddles, shout horrible insults at us and mock us when we practise...

But we soldier on, ignoring them as best we can. The harder we practise, the more likely we are to win our freedom!

It isn't the greatest place to live. The beds are hard and the food is DISGUSTING! (Unless, of course, you're Felix.)

But we're grateful still to be alive and we all really want to win our freedom so we can see our families and friends again!

After weeks of intense work, we are beefed up and ready for our first fight!

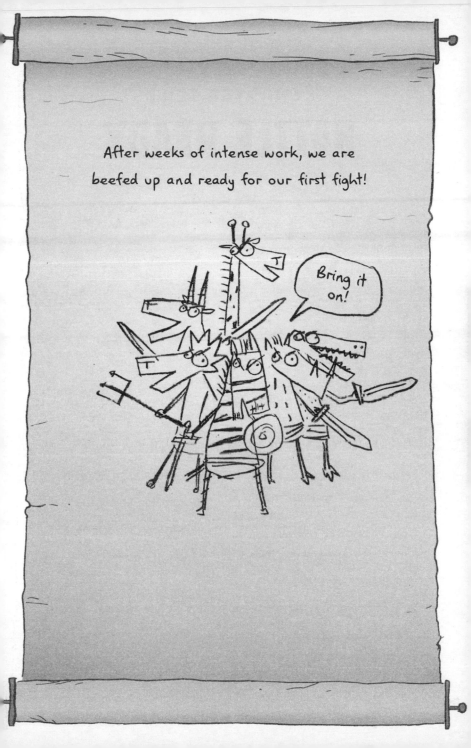

CHAPTER TEN
BATTLE READY

The school's noisy cockerel woke up Julius and his fellow trainee gladiators, just as it had every sunrise for the past month. But today, instead of the usual resistance to getting out of bed, there was a great sense of nervous excitement and urgency in their small barracks.

Felix was so distracted he didn't even bother giving his rock collection its morning polish.

FELIX'S ROCK COLLECTION

They scoffed down their porridge as if it was the
tastiest breakfast ever. Even happily chomping on
crunchy beetles, as if they were
juicy raisins sweetening the gruel.

Today was the big rehearsal,
designed to show Hadrian they would be
ready for his birthday bash. It was also the first time
they would get to fight actual *proper* gladiators! No
more poking swords at wooden poles, or having to
do twenty star jumps for forgetting their nappy. This
was the REAL DEAL!

After gulping down their breakfast, they rushed
into the school arena, and lined up for inspection.

"RIGHT! YOU STINKY HERD OF HOOVED
WEIRDOS!" bellowed Septimus, striding over, while
his two assistants dragged a large wooden trunk
behind him.

Um ... I don't
have hooves,
I have CLAWS.

"BE QUIET! THAT STILL MAKES YOU A
WEIRDO!" Septimus barked. "So! Finally the day
has arrived when we discover whether a flea-ridden
bunch of no-good ratbags, such as yourselves, are
worthy to bear the name GLADIATOR!"

Septimus strolled out in front of them with his hands behind his back. "Of course, you won't be entering the arena with training swords and shields. Oh no! You'll be needing PROPER weapons, weapons such as the gladius sword – SCOURGE of the Roman army. Or, perhaps, the trident and net – befitting the more nimble among you—"

Before he could finish his sentence, Septimus was barged to the floor in a cloud of dust, as the animals raced to get to the trunk first.

"THIS ISN'T SOME CHILD'S DRESSING-UP GAME!" screamed a furious Septimus. "LINE UP IN THE CENTRE OF THE ARENA IMMEDIATELY!"

"Now you listen to me, you detestable collection of goons!" raged Septimus, dusting himself down. His face contorted like a lion chewing twenty angry wasps. "This isn't some hilarious joke! You're not here as some kind of MONKEY CIRCUS ACT!" He thrust his finger into Julius's face. "Hadrian himself will be watching you this afternoon AND I DEMAND DISCIPLINE!!!"

Suddenly Julius's face also began to contort – his eyebrows twisting and his lips pouting. "Ooh!" he hooted, just like a monkey. "AGH! OOH! OOH!" And he flung his arms around, scratching his armpits and his belly.

Then all the other animals started hopping about and hooting like mad monkeys, too.

"RIGHT! THAT'S IT!" shouted Septimus. "NO ONE MAKES A MOCKERY OF ME! I'M CHUCKING YOU ALL IN WITH THE LIONS. I DON'T CARE WHAT HADRIAN SAYS!!"

"A-ANTS!" spluttered Julius, desperately trying to scratch his back. "B-B-BITING ANTS!!"

Septimus strode over to the trunk that had held the gladiator equipment, only to find it swarming with red insects. "WHO DID THIS? WHO PUT THESE ANTS IN HERE?!"

From the first-floor gallery came the unmistakable sound of giggling and guffawing. Septimus whipped round to see Victorius and his fellow gladiators chuckling and slapping one another on the back.

"Well," said Victorius, stifling a laugh. "They were all *itching* to start, so we thought we'd help them along a bit!"

"GAH!" cried an exasperated Septimus, throwing up his arms and marching out of the arena. "Hadrian will be here in half an hour. I haven't got time for this CHILDISH NONSENSE!"

He came back with two big buckets of water and gave them to his assistants. "Wash the ants off these idiots and the equipment. I want everything ready by the time the Emperor arrives! QUICK, QUICK!"

Julius was FUMING! Not only was he covered in very itchy red bites, but he was soaked to the skin in freezing cold water, too! This was meant to be an exciting day to show off their new skills and now it had been RUINED by those muscle-headed berks!

Victorius leaned over the balcony and shouted at the shivering Julius, "Who are the dancing monkeys now, eh?! Ha ha ha!"

Julius spat out a mouthful of cold water and drowned ants, shaking a wet hoof angrily at Victorius. "It was *JUGGLING* monkeys! *JUGGLING*!"

One thing was certain: Julius was not going to forget *this* in a hurry…

CHAPTER ELEVEN

FIRST BLOOD

The small school arena was soon bustling with important dignitaries and curious spectators. All were excited finally to see the famous zebra and his fellow beasts in action. Unbeknown to Julius and his friends, Rome had been talking about little else since his fight with Victorius.

Tickets, normally free for such events, were passing hands for very high prices – with the cost of some seats equalling a whole year's income for a shopkeeper!

In the barracks, little Pliny the mouse was giving the gang a big pep talk. "Now remember what you've been taught! Keep those bodies behind the shield, don't swing your sword wildly and NEVER blink! Don't EVER take your eyes off the enemy, or you'll be DONE FOR!"

And don't forget you are ANIMALS!

Play to your strengths!

Milus was sitting on his bed, carefully cleaning his trident. "We must be cautious," he muttered. "Today is just a showpiece for Hadrian, but these gladiators will be aiming to hurt us. They may be regarded as the lowest of the lows in Roman society, but gladiators are very proud of their sport and we are the unwelcome beetles in their porridge."

Julius had a sudden wave of nerves. "What if they completely thrash us?" he gulped. "We don't stand a chance in the Birthday Games if we can't win a rehearsal! We'll be dog food for CERTAIN!"

Felix stood up. "Listen, guys, I vote that if we lose we try and make a run for it. I'm not hanging around knowing I'm going to be bashed to a pulp."

There was a ripple of agreement – but Pliny was *furious.* "OI, OI ,OI! There'll be no escaping on *my* watch! Just put on a good show to impress Hadrian; that's all that matters today. We'll worry about the Birthday Games later. Trust me!"

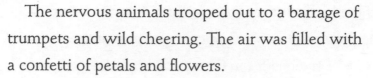

The nervous animals trooped out to a barrage of
trumpets and wild cheering. The air was filled with
a confetti of petals and flowers.

"Wow. They really love us!" Julius whispered to
Cornelius, while waving back to the crowd.

But as they cheerfully paraded around the arena lapping up the applause, from the opposite end strode out the gladiators – also to a great roar of approval.

"We aren't the only popular ones…" replied Cornelius.

They all took their places in the front row of the arena, right next to one another.

On the opposite side, Hadrian sat in his specially decked-out viewing box, furnished with all sorts of splendid silks and gold. He was deep in conversation with Septimus, who was by his side looking quite nervous and agitated.

The trumpets blew again and Septimus quickly stood up. He thrust his arms into the air. "Citizens of Rome! You are about to witness a unique exhibition of gladiatorial combat!

"For the past month, we have taken these lowly beasts and, at Hadrian's bidding, trained them to the highest level!

"So, prepare yourselves for MAN VERSUS BEAST! LET THE GAMES BEGIN!"

Both groups of gladiators moved into position and faced each other.

A man sporting a white tunic with two red stripes running down the front marched in, holding a long stick. It was the Summa Rudis – the referee.

He welcomed the spectators.

"*Gregatim?* What's that?" whispered Julius.

"He means he wants a group fight," Cornelius explained. "We'll probably be acting out some ancient battle. The Romans love that kind of thing."

"Over 150 years ago," continued the Summa Rudis, "our glorious leader, Julius Caesar, conquered the barbarian hordes of Gaul at Alesia! A historic event which will be recreated today before your VERY EYES!"

The trumpets blew and the Summa Rudis waved the two groups off to opposite ends, where they each found a costume box.

"I knew it!" grumped Cornelius, rummaging through the trunk and pulling out a big lump of matted hair. "We DO have to wear stupid moustaches!"

Pliny sneaked over to give them a last boost of morale. "Good work, lads. You look magnificent!"

"And don't worry," Pliny continued. "This group fight makes no difference to your training. Keep your body shielded and your eyes on the enemy. Ain't no way you can fail! Show Hadrian what you're made of!"

As they turned round to make their way back to the centre of the arena, they discovered it had been hastily transformed into a makeshift battleground, with fake trees and rocks and wooden ramps disguised as grassy hillocks.

"Oh, come on, misery guts!" huffed Rufus. "We may as well enjoy ourselves. Let's give this crowd a good show!" And with that, he leapt into the centre of the arena, swinging his sword around and hopping about on his lanky legs as if he were fighting an invisible enemy.

The crowd rose to its feet and cheered at the prancing giraffe. This was what they'd come to see! What peculiar but wonderful animals! The rest of the gang ran to join him and began warming up with their own little routines. And when everyone caught sight of Július, they were in raptures!

Julius didn't disappoint. He twirled his sword into the air, throwing the crowd into even greater thralls of excitement. "Ha ha! Maybe we *can* do this!" he shouted confidently.

A burst of trumpets heralded the start of their fight.

Milus quickly gathered everyone around him.

"Keep tight," he said. "Don't let them pick you off.

We'll be stronger if we stay together."

CLUMP! CLUMP!

CLUMP! CLUMP!

CLUMP!

CLUMP!

CLUMP!

Out of the silence came a
sudden loud thumping sound,
which reverberated around the
arena. *CLUMP! CLUMP! CLUMP!*
CLUMP!

Felix could barely cope with the suspense.
"By the gods! That's them, isn't it?! They're coming!
THEY'RE COMING!! WE'RE ALL GOING TO
DIE!!!"

"STAY CALM!" commanded Milus, keeping his
gaze focused ahead.

"Anyway, we're NOT all going to die," piped up
Cornelius, also fiercely fixing his eyes on the enemy.
"Hadrian still wants us for his birthday bash, doesn't
he?"

"Yes, but whatever happens it's definitely going
to hurt!" whimpered Felix, now a gibbering jelly of a
wreck.

"Well, there is that," conceded Cornelius.

"ARGH!" he cried out suddenly, clutching his face.

Julius quickly turned to his friend, fearing the

worst. "Are you all right? Have you been hit by an arrow?!"

"No, no. It's this blasted moustache. It keeps falling off!"

"This is it!" said Milus. "Here they come!" He clenched his trident just that little bit tighter.

"I-I-I can't do this…" gibbered Felix. "I'm not a gladiator, I'm an ANTELOPE!" He was shaking so hard that his helmet fell over his eyes.

CLUMP!

CLUMP!

CLUMP! CLUMP! CLUMP!

"Hold it together," said Rufus. "It's not like us giraffes are cut out for this sort of thing, either."

"EXACTLY!" spluttered Felix. "We normally RUN at the slightest sign of trouble! Even a gust of wind whistling through a bush sets us off!"

"HOLD YOUR PLACE!" roared Milus.

Suddenly, the row of Romans let out a great roar and charged at the nervous troop of animals.

"NOT ME, I'M OFF!" screamed Felix, chucking his sword and shield in the air and legging it straight out through the exit.

"GAH! FORGET THAT CRETIN!" raged Milus. "BRACE YOURSELVES! BRACE YOURSELVES!!"

The crowd cheered with excitement as the two
armies clashed. It wasn't exactly an accurate depiction
of the Battle of Alesia – these things never were – but
the audience relished it none the less.

On the front bench, Pliny was trying to keep track of
his team, but there was so much dirt being scuffed up,

in such big clouds, it was difficult to make out *anything* that was going on. He shouted out instructions anyway, in the hope that someone might hear.

In the middle of the chaos, Milus attempted to keep the Romans at bay. Fortunately his skills with a trident were second to none.

GRAGH!

KLANG!

Behind him, Julius, Cornelius, Rufus and Lucia tried their best, but they were no match for the veteran fighters.

"I-I can't keep them off any longer...!" cried Cornelius, exhausted. "Pliny was wrong – this is *nothing* like what we trained for!"

"My flipping *arm* hurts!" moaned Rufus. "All I'm doing is banging my sword against their shields. How is this *fair*?"

Seeing things falling apart, Julius tried to rally the troops. "Don't slash your swords!" he shouted. "Poke, remember?!"

This gave Rufus the right hump. "I'll poke *you* if you don't stop bossing everyone around! Just because you got the loudest cheer!"

Julius spun round. "And what's *that* supposed to mean?"

Poor Cornelius began to get lost in a flurry of swords. "Guys! Guys! Try fighting the enemy, not each other!!"

But it was too late. A big swing from one of the Roman swords clobbered Cornelius right on his helmet, sending him flying.

"OH, NO! CORNELIUS!" cried Lucia. But she too took a hit as the deluge of Roman swords finally overpowered her.

With Julius and Rufus bickering at the back, this left just Milus fighting the enemy. But even *his* mighty skills couldn't hold back the tidal wave of blows, and he was sent packing as well.

"Come on, Rufus – it's just you and me!" exclaimed Julius, realizing everyone else was out for the count.

One of the Romans stepped forward. It was, of course, Victorius. "Your lofty friend has hightailed it. A wise option."

He was right. Rufus had legged it.

"It's just you and us now."

Everyone jumped to their feet, chanting, "ZEBRA! ZEBRA! ZEBRA!"

"Come on, then," goaded Julius, fired up by the crowd. He raised his sword.

"No, zebra…" replied Victorius, flatly. "You are not." And with that, he shoved his big shield into Julius's face. Then, with a swing of his sword, he swiped Julius's legs and tipped him over onto his back.

The Summa Rudis marched up to Victorius, grabbed his hand and held it aloft. "THE WINNERS!"

Poor Pliny sat hunched over with his face in his paws. It was a complete disaster! ABSOLUTELY USELESS! They had learned NOTHING!

The crowd were also unimpressed, loudly booing and chucking rotten vegetables at Julius and the others as they attempted to scramble away. This was not the heroes' return they'd been expecting!

Over in Hadrian's box, things were even more serious. The Emperor was red with rage! He had an angry mob on his hands and it was all Septimus's fault!

"They'll be ready, Hadrian! I promise!!" the Lanista reassured him.

"They had better be!" snapped Hadrian. "Or you'll find yourself in a POENA CULLEI!"

CHAPTER TWELVE
THE GREAT ESCAPE

Back in the barracks, while everyone nursed their bumps and bruises, Felix frantically jumped up and down, shouting at everyone. "We HAVE to leave and we have to leave NOW!" he screamed, waving his arms above his head. "If we stay here, we're dead! DEAD!"

A tiny figure scurried into the room.

Felix stood up to protest. "Now you listen to me, Pliny! We weren't prepared for a big fight like that! We were trained as individual gladiators, not a troop of soldiers!"

Pliny put his little paws on his hips, furrowed his brow and looked Felix right in the eye. "And what would *you* know about it, eh? You ran like a flea from a dead rat!"

"Hadrian himself is on the warpath after such an HORRIFIC display! No *true* gladiator would run from the battle, no matter what the fight! At least those who stayed and fought can retain a smidgen of honour."

Suddenly, the barracks door crashed open, almost getting ripped off its hinges. In the entrance stood a red-faced Septimus, contorted with rage. "WHAT IN THE NAME OF JUPITER'S FIERY BEARD WAS THAT?!" he screeched.

Dumbstruck with fear, no one dared talk. Or move. Well – apart from Felix, who felt his point still needed to be made. He raised a hoof and stood up. "Look, Septimus. As I was just saying to Pliny, it really was unfair to expect—"

But before he could finish his sentence, Septimus grabbed Felix, dragged him to the doorway and booted him so hard up the bottom that he flew high out of the school and into the clouds. No one was left in any doubt that Felix was well on his way to the forests of Germania.

Septimus turned to face the rest of the cowering creatures. "ANYBODY ELSE FEEL THEY'VE GOT SOMETHING TO ADD TO THIS DISCUSSION?"

"GOOD! NOW, GIVE ME 100 STAR JUMPS AND 20 LAPS ROUND THE ARENA. HOP TO IT! COME ON!!"

"And when you're finished, we can discuss the WORLD OF PAIN I've got planned for your training regime and last pathetic week on this earth!"

Julius leapt up and down. His weary muscles, battered and bruised limbs and painfully sore ant bites reminded him that today was probably the worst day of his life. Fact. "There's only so much more I can take of this!" he said under his breath, grimacing.

Lucia star-jumped her way over to him. "Don't worry," she whispered. "I've thought of an amazing plan! If all goes well, we could be on our way home by the morning." She tapped her nose and, with a wink of her eye, star-jumped back to where she'd come from.

HUP! HUP! HUP!

BOING! BOING!

That evening, as the lamps went out in the Ludus Magnus, Lucia crept round the tiny barracks, tapping everyone on their feet as they lay in their beds.

Tiptoeing like tiny mice, Julius and the others followed Lucia to the school's outer perimeter wall.

To their surprise, Rufus was already there, hiding in the shadows. And as they got closer, it was suddenly apparent that he was still wearing his Gaul-fighting costume from their disastrous battle. Moustache and all!

"Wait! What's going on?!" exclaimed Julius.

"Hush!" said Lucia. "Put this on."

She handed each of them a fake moustache.

Bah. How I hate these things.

"I don't get it… Why are we dressing up as Gauls again?" Julius whispered as he pulled on a pair of checked trousers.

"Because that's how Rufus and I disguise ourselves when we sneak out to watch the chariot racing," replied Lucia. "We found that costume box weeks ago. No one has ever stopped us or given us a second look when we're dressed up. We'll just wear these costumes and stroll right out through the main gate. No problem!"

Suddenly all Lucia's and Rufus's mysterious absences from training made sense.

Enough of this talk. If we're to leave, we must leave now!

"But what about Pliny?" asked Julius. "Shouldn't he come along, too, after everything he's done for us?"

"Forget the mouse," growled Milus. "He can come and go as he pleases. He'll soon find some other idiots to talk to."

Julius wasn't convinced. "We should at least say goodbye. He's worked so hard with us."

Milus grabbed Julius by the moustache. "Listen, zebra. If we don't leave now, we'll be caught and any chance we had of getting home will be lost!"

"Yes, come on," said Rufus. "If Septimus catches us out here, we'll be star-jumping till sunrise."

Lucia quietly leapt onto Rufus's back and climbed up his neck.

This way! Quickly!

And with that, she disappeared over the wall and off into the shadows.

The others quickly followed.

It was no easy task grappling their way up Rufus's slippery neck. Cornelius even fell off a couple of times. But they were desperate to escape and happy to get away by any means necessary.

Once they'd eventually scrambled over the wall, they crouched in the darkness next to Lucia.

"Wait," whispered Julius. "How's Rufus going to climb up here? Isn't he coming?"

"But I'm right here!" came Rufus's voice, directly behind him.

Julius nearly jumped out of his skin! "What the…? Where did *you* come from?"

"Where *did* you come from?" he continued in a whisper. "I didn't see you climb over the wall!"

Rufus pointed back down the street. "I used that little door – it connects the road directly to the barracks. Quite handy, really."

"You IMBECILE!" snarled Milus. "We could've ALL used that! Why didn't you tell the rest of us?"

Rufus looked quite hurt. "Well, where's the fun in that? I thought it would be exciting to make a daring escape up a giraffe's neck. Something to tell your grandchildren about!"

"Shh!" said Lucia. "Someone's coming!"

Everybody slipped back into the shadows and kept very still.

"Uh-oh. Now we're for it," whispered Cornelius. "I think he saw us."

"FELIX!?" they all gasped.

"Yep, it's me!" he said gleefully. "Where are you all off to? Are you finally making the Big Getaway?"

"Wait a minute, shouldn't you have been booted all the way to Germania?" asked Cornelius.

"Well, I didn't quite make it *that* far, but I did end up over the city wall! It was quite a task getting back in here, I can tell you."

"But why have you come back?" puzzled Cornelius.

"To escape, of course! We can't hang around here any longer. 'Only death awaits us!'"

"You fool, Felix!" rasped Milus. "You'd already escaped! You didn't need to come back!"

"Oh, yeah..." Felix pondered a moment. "I never thought about it like that. Oh well, I'm here now!" he said cheerfully. "What's the plan?"

Lucia gave him a spare moustache. "Just put this on and keep your voice down. We're heading for the main gate and sneaking out disguised as Gauls."

She crept into the road, checked that the coast was clear, then beckoned everyone to follow.

Felix scampered up to her while sticking on his itchy moustache. "What I will say, though, is try and avoid the Circus Maximus. There's a HUGE chariot race going on. THOUSANDS of people are milling around. I think even Hadrian *himself* is there tonight."

Lucia skidded to a halt, eyes bulging. She slapped herself on the forehead. "By the GODS! In all the haste to escape, I'd completely forgotten! Tonight is the Grand Final between the Whites and the Greens!"

We have to go. I can't miss it!

Julius put his hoof on Lucia's shoulder. "Lucia, we can't take the risk. If we start mingling with the crowds, we'll be found out *for sure.*"

Lucia gazed blankly at the floor and wiped a tear from her eye. "I know..." she sighed, looking up at Julius and sniffing.

He smiled and patted her on the back. "You know it's for the best."

Then, looking him right in the eye, she said, "I-I'm sorry, Julius..."

"Sorry? Sorry for what?"

And Lucia shot off up the road as fast as her little legs could carry her.

"She ... SHE BIT ME! Lucia actually BIT ME!!" whimpered Julius, holding his arm.

"Well, she *is* a crocodile," said Cornelius. "Biting zebras is kinda what they do."

"Cor, she's keen on those chariots, isn't she!" remarked Felix.

"Lucia's desperate to become a charioteer," explained Rufus, who'd always escaped with her to the races. "And she's got a real passion for the Green team. If they finally beat those rotten Whites tonight, it will be a sensation!"

Milus suddenly erupted with impatience. "AARGH! You lot TALK TOO MUCH!" And in a great huff, he ran off after Lucia!

Everyone just stood there, shocked.

"Well, how rude," said Felix.

"We'd better try and catch them," said Julius. "If we start getting split up, it's only going to cause more trouble."

As he and the others approached the Circus Maximus, they were indeed greeted by large crowds.

"Bah! We'll never find them now," puffed
Cornelius. "We should just cut our losses and make a
run for it."

"This way!" said Rufus. "We always go through
this little entrance. It has the best view!"

"I think you probably have the best view *wherever* you sit, Rufus!" said Julius.

True.

As they barged their way through the bustle of spectators, Julius scanned the crowd for Lucia and Milus. There was a mad cocktail of people from all over Rome and the Empire beyond. Street sellers sat next to senators, who sat next to goat farmers, who sat next to centurions.

Everyone was singing and shouting about their favourite horses.

This is the closest to the smelly chaos of the watering hole back home I've ever seen, thought Julius.

A great "OOOH!" went round the seats as one of the charioteers crashed, his chariot wheels exploding into smithereens.

"Cor, this is actually quite exciting!" said Felix, hypnotized by the crazy scene. "Does anybody know what's happening?"

Cornelius let out a little cough. "Well, my dear antelope, what you have here are four teams of charioteers – Red, Green, Blue and White…"

"Argh!" cried Julius. "We haven't got time for one of your fact sessions!"

"Oh, hush now," scolded Cornelius, carrying on. "They speed round the track seven times…"

"Why do I bother?" Julius mumbled, throwing his arms in the air.

Just then, amongst the rabble, Julius spotted Lucia. "THERE!" he pointed. "I'd recognize that moustache anywhere!"

He and the others jostled their way through the spectators towards their friend. She was happily watching the race; Milus was nowhere to be seen.

"Lucia! It's us! Where's Milus? Is he with you?"

But Lucia was deep in conversation and didn't look up.

"Oh, don't be mad with me, Lucia," said Julius, as they all squished in on the crowded seats. "I forgive you for chomping my arm. Anyway, who's your new friend? Aren't you going to introduce us?"

Julius's face was a picture of horror: his mouth dropped to the floor.

Felix whispered in Julius's ear, "What's with Lucia's mad accent? Is that meant to be Gaulish? Sounds more like a yodelling hippo!"

"It's not the accent I'm worried about," said Julius. "Look who she's talking to – it's Dead Bird Hat Man!"

Felix stifled a scream.

The centurion leaned over. "Very nice to meet you," he said. "I'm a big fan of your cheese and wine. A very welcome addition to our glorious Empire!"

Julius bowed and smiled, keeping his head down. "We need to get away NOW," he hissed. "Or we can say goodbye to any hope of escaping! Come ON!" He nodded and winked towards Dead Bird Hat Man.

"Is there something wrong with your eye?" Lucia asked. "Now, if you don't mind, my friend and I would like to finish watching the race."

Felix and Cornelius joined in on the nodding and winking now.

"Are your friends annoying you?" asked Dead Bird Hat Man. "If they are, I can quite easily arrange for them to be thrown into the arena."

"Ahem. No, eet eez nuthink," replied Lucia in her best Gaulish accent. "They was just leafing anyways." And she turned and gave them all the iciest of stares.

"Yes!" snapped Julius. "And YOU'RE coming with us!"

They all grabbed her and hauled her off her seat.

"GUYS! PLEASE PUT ME DOWN! I WANT TO WATCH THE RACE!" She wriggled and squirmed, trying to get free.

Time seemed to stand still as the centurion sat agog at the moustache-free face of Julius – and Julius stared back, frozen with fear, knowing the game was up.

"YOU!!!" screamed the centurion. "THE STRIPY IDIOT! GUARDS! GUARDS! ARREST THESE BEASTS! ARREST THEM!!"

As the Roman guards raced towards the animals, Lucia turned to a despairing Julius. "Oh! He was *that* horrible centurion! I thought I recognized him. Well, WHY didn't you tell me?"

Julius rolled his eyes in frustration. Their master plan for staying alive had been foiled. Completely. And now they were being hustled back to the Ludus Magnus to await their inevitable fate.

CHAPTER THIRTEEN
THE CHAMPION OF CHAMPIONS!

A week later, Emperor Hadrian's birthday was finally upon Rome and the whole city was bursting with sounds and colour! Ornate banners and flower garlands hung from every window down every street – streets that fizzed with the singing and dancing of happy citizens!

The biggest, loudest celebrations of all came from the Colosseum. It always roared with excitement, but today it was rammed to the rafters with the highest of spirits! Every dancing bear was deafeningly cheered; every juggling monkey (Yes! There WERE juggling monkeys!) was applauded till the walls of the stadium rattled.

When Rome threw a party, it REALLY threw a party and everyone – from senator to slave – was determined to have the best time of their lives!

But deep in the bowels of the Colosseum, the atmosphere was far from festive. Julius and his friends sat staring at the floor, barely looking up. Their mood was as solemn as a funeral, even when a great roar from the crowd shook the ceiling and crumbled plaster on their heads.

"Well, it's been nice knowing you all," sighed a despondent Felix.

SHUT UP, FELIX!

"Look," said Julius. "We know we're all going to die, but we'd rather you'd just zip it."

"Come on!" said Cornelius, swishing his sword. "We can DO this! All our extra training this week has turned us into LEAN, MEAN, FIGHTING MACHINES!"

But no one took any notice.

"We don't stand a chance against the might of the Empire's great gladiatorial champions," Milus growled from the shadows. "We may as well just lie down and let them finish us off, once and for all."

Julius sighed, cursing himself for getting into such a rotten mess all those weeks ago. How could he have been so stupid as to think he could gallivant off on his own like that? He'd give anything to be with his family now. "Perhaps they'll come to rescue me after all," he hoped, aloud.

"You bet your life they're trying to find you," said Cornelius. "Maybe my family are trying to find me, too..."

Just then, little Pliny waltzed in. "Well, this is cheery," he said, checking out the grim faces.

Although I can't say I'm surprised, coming from a band of QUITTERS!

Pliny was still annoyed at them all for trying to escape and NOT TELLING HIM! Not even his old pal, Milus. Oh, yes, Milus. The worst escape artist in Rome's long, glorious history. He had been back at the barracks sooner than the others – picked up by a patrol just outside the Colosseum.

Look, Pliny, we're sorry about last week...

Talk to the hand, 'cos the mouse ain't listening.

"You'd better pull your sorry finger out, 'cos you're up against some pretty tough opponents today," Pliny said.

"I fear nothing!" Cornelius declared triumphantly. "Not while I wear my lucky Subligaria!"

"Lucky? How can a nappy be *lucky*?!" snorted Julius.

"Well," said Cornelius, sidling up to him. "I'm glad you asked."

Julius let out a low sigh.

"Now, today is the Vernal Equinox…" Cornelius began.

"The … what? It *is*?" Julius puzzled.

"Indeed it is. This is when daytime and night-time are of equal length – something the gods view *very* favourably…"

"Wait a minute," piped up Felix. "If it's the er … Vernon Equiplops, or whatever it's called, surely it's lucky for *everybody*?"

"Aha!" boasted Cornelius. "This is where the gods were smiling on *me* in particular. As I was pulling my nappy on this morning, a little frog hopped past, croaking as he went. *That*, my friends, is a sign from the gods themselves that they wish me happiness and good fortune."

But before Cornelius could reply, a figure appeared in the doorway. "Farewell, you incompetent buffoons." It was, of course, Septimus. "I can't be too harsh on you, though. You've earned me a pretty penny just by lasting long enough till today."

He walked over and eyed them with his ferocious gaze.

"If by some miracle you do survive, which you won't, *never* darken my doors with your fetid, stinking, ugly faces again."

And off he went, as suddenly as he'd appeared, slamming the door behind him.

"You know, I think I'm going to miss that scraggy old face," said Felix.

"I'll say one thing for him, though," said Julius. "He always did smell rather lovely."

A great blaring of trumpets was followed by an enormous roar.

As the dust settled, Julius felt his stomach sink as if down a great well. "This is it!" he said.

❦ CHAPTER FOURTEEN ❧
SHOWTIME!

The door swung open for a final time. It was the
Dungeon Master. "Right, you lot, up to the main
entrance. I like to keep it very clean up there. No
pooing on the floor!"

Don't worry! We're wearing nappies!

So off they trotted, up the stairwell and along the
dark corridors, threading under the arena.

A welcome, cool breeze greeted them as they
reached a great arch. But a stench wafted on the air –
the stench of sweating, stinking, hulking gladiators.
The gladiators' armour creaked and their shields
scraped against the walls as they all turned round.

"Don't forget the Golden Rules!" shouted Pliny,
scampering behind them. "And be yourselves!
Honestly, it will save your lives!"

This really *is it,* thought Julius as the great gate
swung open to a cacophony of cheers and trumpets.
He gulped hard. *My fate awaits me...*

And the gladiators all began to make their way out
of the darkness and into the Colosseum.

"GOOD LUCK!" Pliny called out. "I'M GOING TO
MISS YOU GUYS!"

Hadrian stood up to greet his birthday bashers. The stage was finally set for the Champion of Champions!

In the centre of the amphitheatre the Summa Rudis took his place. He raised his hand above his head – and everyone fell silent.

"CITIZENS OF ROME!" he bellowed. "TODAY YOU BEAR WITNESS TO THE MOST GLORIOUS OF GAMES! GLADIATORS FROM ACROSS OUR GREAT AND NOBLE EMPIRE WILL DO BATTLE FOR THE TITLE OF 'CHAMPION OF CHAMPIONS' AND THEIR FREEDOM!"

The roar of the crowd rattled through Julius's armour, and his knees knocked together with nerves. He tried to push thoughts of failure to the back of his mind.

Whatever happens today, he thought, *I want to make sure I fight with honour. If word ever does get back to Mum and Brutus, I want them to know I was a true zebra – not the useless wimp they knew before.*

He quickly scanned the audience for their familiar stripy faces, but neither of them was there.

The RULES are very simple:
1. This is a knockout tournament.
2. There will be only one winner.
3. No cheating – or you will be thrown to THE LIONS!

The Summa Rudis approached the gladiators' bench and summoned Cornelius and a mountain of a man, called Destroius, to the stage.

"Argh! I can't watch!" cried Felix.

"Good luck, Cornelius!" shouted Julius. "Remember your lucky nappy!"

Cornelius strode out defiantly. He was *very* keen to show off his new skills. He also felt particularly smart in his gladiator get-up.

Cornelius fixed his gaze on Destroius, who stood

in stony silence waiting for the signal to start.

The trumpets parped and Destroius went straight in with a big swing of his axe, slashing the air above the plucky little warthog, who quickly ducked out of the way.

Cornelius danced around, thrusting his weapon and barking, "POKE POKE!" before catching Destroius in the armpit with his sword.

The crowd leapt to their feet, cheering.

"GO ON, CORNELIUS!" screamed Julius.

"KEEP STILL!!" boomed Destroius as he swung his huge axe a second time, smashing it into the sand as the little hairy beast hopped out of the way.

Julius began to feel hopeful.

He knew warthogs were nippy little fellows, but this was something else! Cornelius was running rings round Destroius!

Cornelius turned to Julius and gave him the thumbs-up. He didn't see the axe hit him.

Everyone was stunned into silence.

"NOOOO!" gasped Julius.

"He … he's flown right out of the arena!" spluttered Rufus.

"Cornelius broke one of the Golden Rules," snarled Milus. "He took his eyes off the enemy." The lion turned to Julius and gave him the sternest of looks. "Some idiot distracted him."

Julius buried his face in his hooves.

"Well, so much for his lucky nappy," gulped Felix.

Next, the Summa Rudis turned to Milus and a gladiator covered head to foot in armour and padding. "You two next!"

Milus picked up his trident and net and strode out to a big cheer from the crowd.

Bring it on...

Never in his wildest dreams had Julius thought he'd want a lion to win a fight as much as he did now.

Milus's opponent was Agrippa. He brandished the menacing weapons of the Scissor Gladiator!

The trumpets blared, the crowd roared and the two enemies snarled into action.

At first they skirted round each other like two crabs in a rock pool.

Then Agrippa thrust his bladed arm at Milus's chest – but Milus skipped out of the way with ease.

They circled each other again.

Occasionally Agrippa slashed the air, inviting Milus to swing his net towards him. But Milus was quick. He leapt like an acrobat, clashing his trident into Agrippa's shoulder before landing nimbly behind him.

The audience rose in awe, cheering each of the wild cat's agile moves.

Even so, Julius remained a bag of nerves.

In a flash, Milus somersaulted – like an arrow shot from a bow – and back-flipped. He pulled his net over Agrippa's helmet and shoulders and clasped the giant's arms tightly to his sides.

"HE'S WON!" shouted Julius, springing up from his seat.

"Wait," said Rufus, calmly. "This isn't over yet."

With a big GRUNT, Agrippa flexed his muscles and threw Milus to the floor. Then he scythed off the net with his knife as if he were brushing off a cobweb.

The crowd gasped.

But Milus wasn't finished *just* yet. Using his trident as if he were doing a pole vault, he booted his opponent's chest, knocking him right off his feet. Agrippa groaned, and Milus braced himself for a final vault to finish him off.

But in his moment of glory, Milus TRIPPED and fell flat on his face in the dirt.

Immediately Agrippa launched onto his back, holding him down and twisting his arm like a wrestler.

"He ... he TRIPPED!" gasped Julius. "But he was just about to win! This is a DISASTER!" He buried his head in his hooves again.

"I think he tripped over Cornelius's lucky nappy," said Rufus. "Milus'll be furious!"

"Forget that. It's all over for Milus now," cried Julius. "I can't bear to watch."

"Hey! Listen!" shouted Lucia. "The crowd's *booing*. They're not letting Agrippa kill Milus!"

Julius peeped through his hooves. It was true! All around the arena the audience were waving white hankies.

"Hadrian's letting him LIVE!" he cried.

"But what will become of *us*?" sniffed Felix, who was fearing the worst.

"We'll worry about that when we get to it," snarled a newly determined Julius.

Just then the Summa Rudis pointed at them both. "You two next!"

"But wait – who are we fighting?" asked Felix.

At the sight of Julius, the crowd were on their feet.

"ZEBRA! ZEBRA! ZEBRA!" they chanted.

"They still love you, then!" Felix remarked.

Julius ignored him and promptly bonked him on the head.

"OI! What are you DOING!?" screamed Felix. "I thought we had a pinky swear?"

"Shut up, you idiot!" whispered Julius. "I'm trying to knock you out. Then I'll refuse to kill you. It's your only chance!" He smacked him again with his sword.

"CAREFUL!" shouted Felix. "That actually flippin' hurt!" Then he took a swing with his own sword, clipping Julius on the nose.

"HEY!" cried Julius, holding his face. "What are you doing?"

"Same as you! I'll knock you out and then promise not to kill *you*." And Felix took another swing.

This time Julius held up his shield. "Listen, you fool," he barked. "If you knock me out, you'll face certain death against those ogres in the next round."

"OK…" Felix paused a moment. "Let me knock *myself* out."

"WHAT?"

"Let me knock myself out. Your bashing hurts too much."

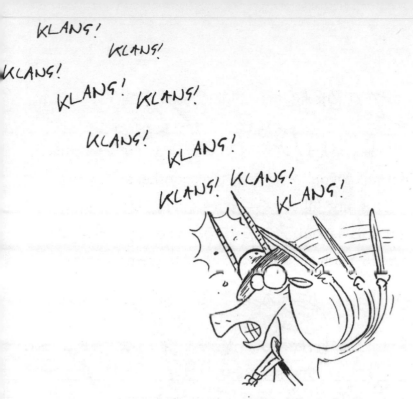

The crowd were outraged! This wasn't a fight! A loud "BOO!" reverberated round the amphitheatre.

"I-I can't do it!" sobbed Felix. "I'm too scared of pain!"

"Oh, for goodness sake!" hissed Julius. And with an almighty swoosh of his sword he walloped Felix to the ground.

The jeers turned to cheers as Julius stood triumphant.

Only Lucia and Rufus remained.

Will they make it past the first round? Julius wondered.

Lucia wasn't the greatest fighter, but she had the distinct advantage of being a crocodile. And her rows of teeth quickly unnerved her opponent, the great swordsman Spurius, who surrendered as soon as she got to grips with him!

Rufus was up against a particularly big brute called Prudes, who fought as a Retiarius, much like Milus – with a net and trident. But Rufus had trained well and, not forgetting the Golden Rules and with a dash of long-legged creativity, eventually beat his opponent, too.

Up in his special imperial box, Emperor Hadrian was revelling in the horror and madness of the show. Septimus sat by his side, supping his wine.

"Ha ha! Good work, Septimus, my friend!" laughed Hadrian, slapping Septimus on the back, making him spill his drink. "This beats ALL my birthday bashes! These animals of yours have SPIRIT!"

"Yes, quite, Hadrian, but they are idiots! I'll be glad when they're gone."

Hadrian grabbed a honey-dipped flamingo tongue from a bowl and popped it into his mouth. "Then you'll be interested to hear about my brilliant idea, my dear Septimus."

Back on the gladiators' bench, Pliny was shouting at Lucia, who was fighting a very skilful swordsman called Attilius.

But poor Lucia couldn't get near her opponent. As Attilius thrust forward with his weapon, Lucia shuffled out of the way – just in time – before panicking and following up with a BIG, crazy swing of her sword.

Pliny went ballistic! "AARGH!! WHAT ARE YOU DOING?!"

But it was too late.

Pliny plopped down on his seat, exasperated, and folded his little arms. "Why do I even bother?" he wailed. "How someone with big chops, full of razor-sharp teeth, can lose a fight is beyond me!"

Rufus was up next.

Julius gave him a big hearty pat on the back. "GOOD LUCK, RUFUS!" he shouted.

"I wouldn't get your hopes too high," Pliny whispered. "He's up against Maximilian, second only to Victorius!"

Julius looked over at Maximilian. He really was a big brute of a man.

"He plays pretty dirty, too," snarled Pliny.

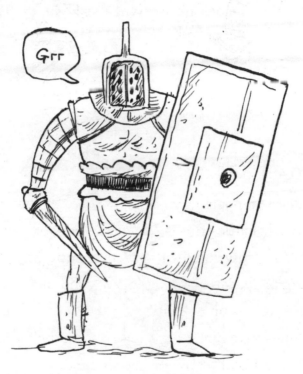

Almost straight away, Maximilian taunted Rufus. "Call yourself a gladiator?" he shouted. "You're more like a bundle of STICKS!"

Rufus didn't like this and started smacking his sword against Maximilian's massive shield.

The muscly gladiator jumped out of the way, laughing. "It must be windy!" he yelled. "Your pathetic branches are swaying weakly in the breeze!"

Rufus's ungainliness was just what Maximilian wanted. He leapt towards the giraffe and STAMPED on his hoof.

STAMP!

"MY TOOTSIES!!!!" screamed Rufus, holding
his hoof.

With Rufus distracted, Maximilian knocked
him clean over into the dust and stood on him,
triumphant!

As the crowd roared, Julius and Pliny sat with
their heads in their hooves and paws.

"I told you!" said Pliny. "He's a nasty one, that
Maximilian!"

This, of course, left Julius as the final animal competitor. He immediately found himself faced with Milus's victor, the slashing Agrippa. But Julius had seen how close Milus had come to beating Agrippa, and went into his fight fired up!

"BE A ZEBRA!!" shouted Pliny.

"BUT I *AM* A ZEBRA!!" Julius shouted back, confused.

"NO, I MEAN USE YOUR ZEBRA SKILLS. AGRIPPA AIN'T EXACTLY SPEEDY!"

Pliny was right. Agrippa was no match for the nimble Julius. He lumbered about the arena, hopelessly slashing the air as the zebra darted back and forth.

It didn't take long for the confident Julius finally to take out the exhausted gladiator.

At last, the crowd had a proper ZEBRA WIN to cheer about!

But his next opponent wasn't going to be so easy to overcome: it was Maximilian.

"Watch him," growled Pliny. "I don't think he's going to be as merciful as the other gladiators, if you get my meaning."

Julius gritted his teeth and bravely faced up to the imposing gladiator.

Ignoring the taunts, Julius held fast, keeping his eyes firmly fixed on his overconfident opponent.

Maximilian attacked Julius with ferocity, but Julius dug in and batted away the pummelling sword.

Up in the imperial box, Hadrian was transfixed. "He really is quite something, this zebra," he cooed.

Even Septimus was pretty impressed. He leaned in close to the Emperor. "From a student of Ludus Magnus, you wouldn't expect anything less."

Hadrian sniffed the air. "For such an arrogant brute, you really do smell of the most exquisite flowers."

Back in the arena, Julius was still standing up to Maximilian, who was now teasing him – lolloping, horse-like, in front of him.

Come on, you prancing pony! Show me what you've got!

"Even a pony wouldn't be so reckless!" shouted Julius, smacking Maximilian's sword clean out of his hand. Julius then inflicted a barrage of pokes on the shocked and weaponless gladiator.

Maximilian flailed and stumbled backwards before falling, unceremoniously, onto his bottom.

Thinking he had won, Julius turned triumphantly to his adoring crowd and punched the air with his hoof.

"LOOK OUT!" cried Pliny from the sidelines.

Julius turned just in time to catch the villainous Victorius kicking a *new* sword across the sand to Maximilian.

"YOU CAN'T LET HIM DO THAT!" screamed Julius.

But the Summa Rudis just waved Julius away.

"Well, we know who pays YOUR wages!" growled the zebra, turning on Maximilian in a ferocious attack. "I'm not letting you steal my chance of freedom THAT easily!" he raged.

A bamboozled Maximilian couldn't fight back and, with a final hefty blow, Julius smacked the dastardly gladiator to the floor.

The crowd went crazy!

Not only had their hero beaten the big cheat, but Julius was now – unbelievably – through to the final!

❧ CHAPTER FIFTEEN ❧
SHOWDOWN

Waiting for Julius in the wings was Pliny the mouse, who brought him some fresh water. "It looks as if it's you and Victorius again. He's been gunning for you since day one and I don't think it's a coincidence he's your opponent in the final. Next time, try keeping your mouth shut when it comes to figuring out who the juggling monkeys are – you get me?"

Julius's other friends came over to gee him on, too.

"Good luck, Julius!" said an elated Cornelius. "You can borrow my lucky nappy if you want."

Julius politely declined.

"I'm sorry that I got you mixed up in this," said Milus, patting Julius on the shoulder. "But perhaps it's been the making of you!"

"Oh, pass me the sick bag!" said Pliny, shoving Milus out of the way.

Julius took a deep breath and closed his eyes. He imagined himself getting a noogie from his stupid brother while their mum shouted at them to stop their nonsense. He opened his eyes again and gritted his teeth. "Right," he said. "Let's do this."

Now, go kick some Roman BUTT!

ZEBRA! ZEBRA! ZEBRA!

And so the two gladiators stood facing each other across the arena.

Victorius, Rome's very own champion – once their greatest hero of all time.

And Julius. Fighting for his life in a world he'd never heard of until a few weeks ago.

Can I be a different kind of zebra? he thought. *Can I prove I'm not just a wimpy nincompoop?*

His thoughts were interrupted by trumpets
blowing for the final time. The crowd erupted.

"Listen, zebra," whispered Victorius above the
noise. "I can do you a deal. Give up now and I will
spare your life. I know of a farm in Hispania. They
have some of the best-kept stables in the Empire.
You only have to say the word and it's yours..."

"NEVER!" shouted Julius and he thrust forward

with a poke of his sword.

Victorius easily parried the weapon away. "Now, don't get cross," he teased. "They accept only the *finest* horses – even *stripy* ones!"

"SHUT UP!" Julius lashed out in a flurry of pokes – each one expertly deflected by Victorius, who continued to goad him.

"And only the sweetest of hay…"

"Roman, you talk too much!" said Julius, thwacking Victorius as hard as he could.

Victorius fell back. But their swords continued to clash and screech together until, with one mighty blow, Julius's sword was sent whizzing through the air, far behind him.

"You are a fool, zebra," shouted Victorius. "I gave you a chance, yet you spurned it. That was a mistake – a mistake you will pay for with your LIFE!"

Julius stumbled. *Uh-oh. This is it,* he thought. *This is the end.*

But as Victorius positioned himself for the killer blow, a voice called out:

Julius caught the sword out of mid-air.

"CHEAT!" cried Victorius, pointing to the stands. "YOU ALL SAW IT! THE LION HELPED HIM!"

As the Roman guards rushed to restrain Milus, he shouted, "Yeah, what are you going to do? Throw me to the lions? I look forward to catching up with some old friends!"

Victorius exploded into a rage! He swiped at Julius, blinded by anger, pounding his shield mercilessly. "WHAT IS IT WITH YOU ANIMALS?" he screamed.

Julius kept his focus. He waited. And he waited. He needed the perfect moment to strike.

Then it came. Victorius, as always, broke the Golden Rule and raised his arm for the final killer blow.

Julius didn't waste a moment.

Victorius was out cold.
Julius slumped to his knees.

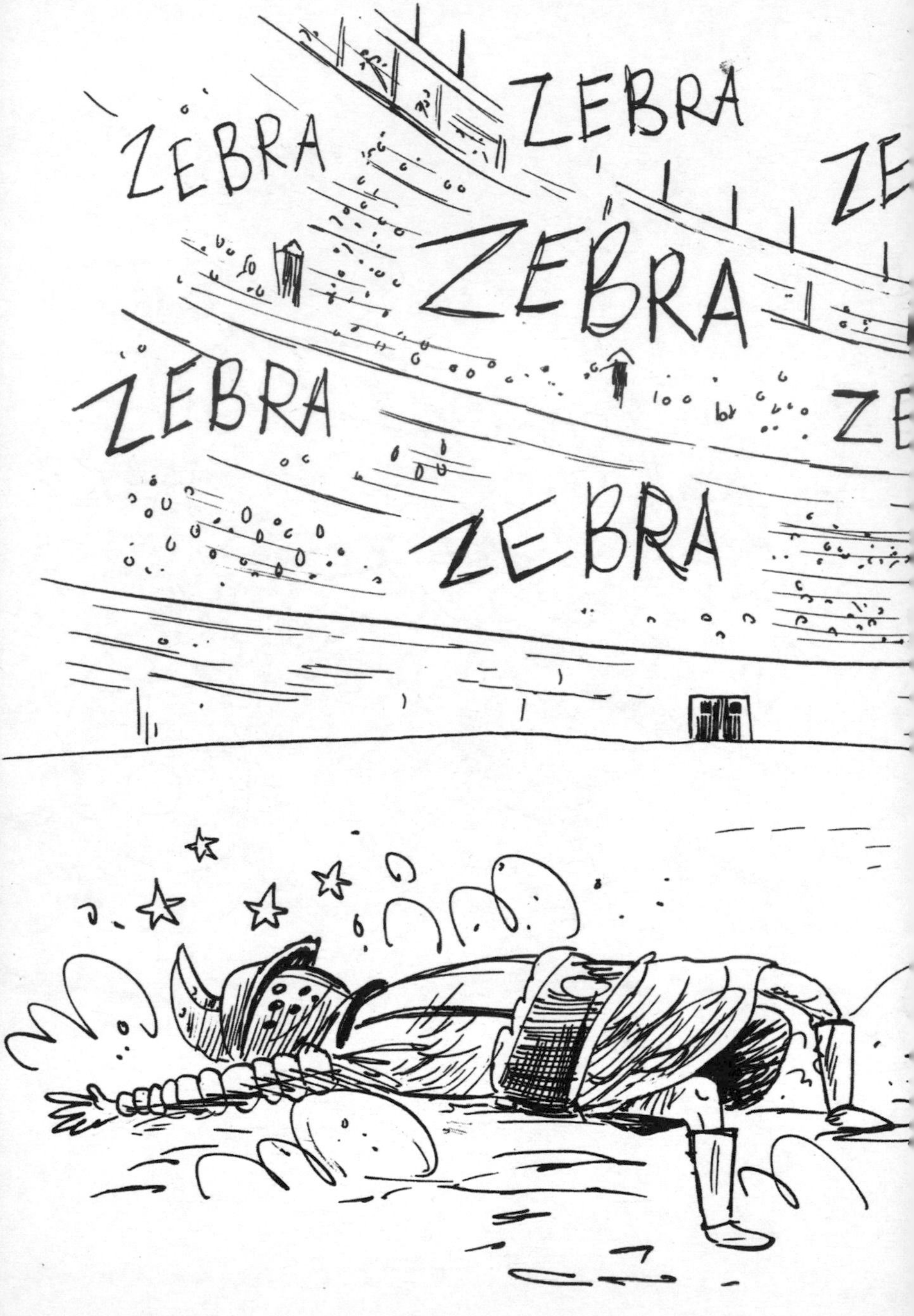
ZEBRA
ZEBRA
ZEBRA
ZEBRA
ZEBRA

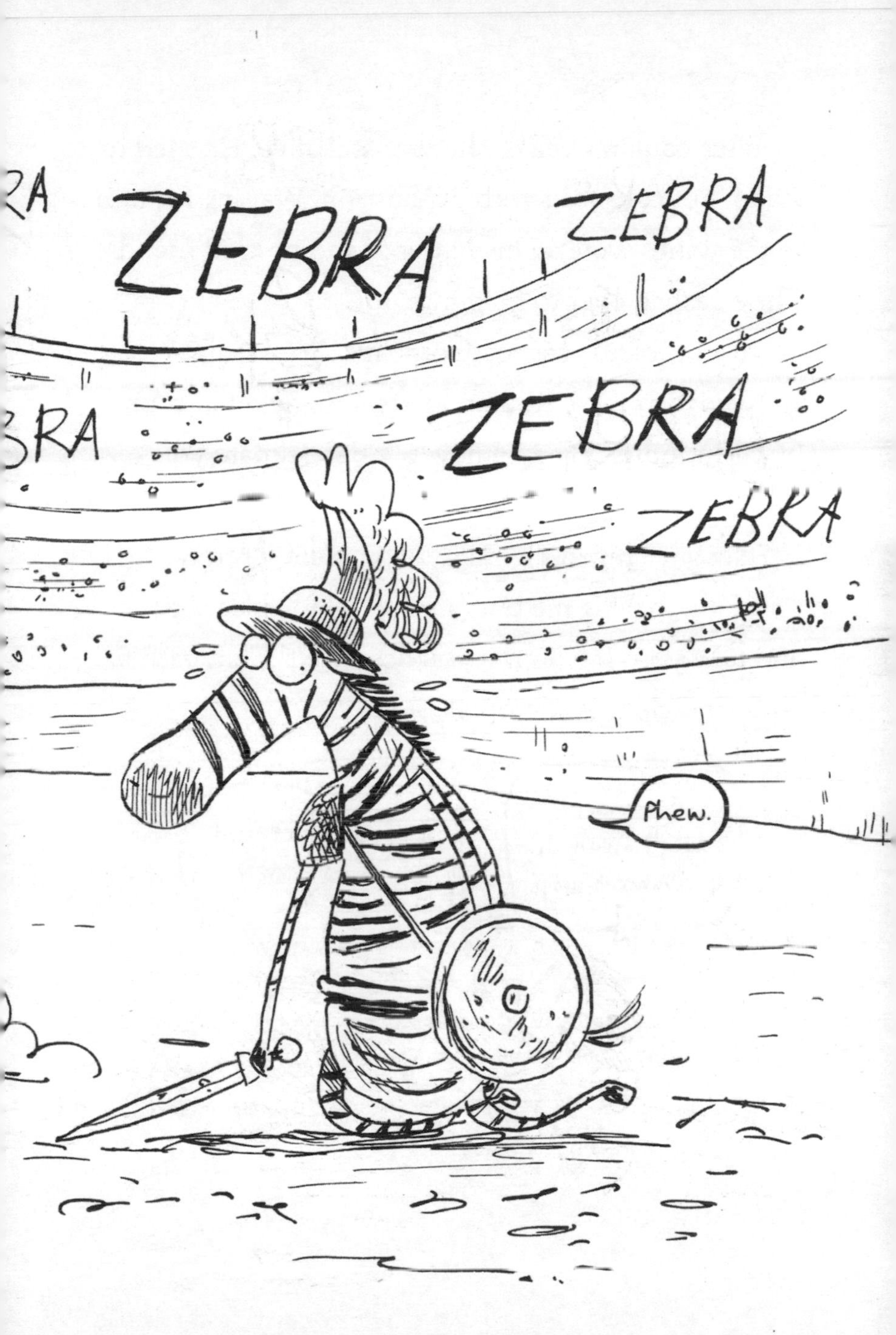
RA
ZEBRA
ZEBRA
BRA
ZEBRA
ZEBRA
Phew.

Julius couldn't believe he was still alive. He tried to stand, but collapsed with exhaustion. Waiting for him in the wings were all his battered and bruised friends. They dashed over to help him up.

"Just brilliant!" gasped Cornelius. "You really showed it to these Roman idiots." He held Julius up by the armpits. "They'll never underestimate you again!"

Felix gave him a big hug. "I completely forgive you for knocking me out (sort of). Now, please go and take your freedom – you deserve it! That path to fame and glory is all yours!"

"But what about you lot? What's going to happen to you now?" Julius wheezed.

Lucia went up to him and gave him a big cuddle. She whispered in his ear, "Don't worry, we have another exciting plan of escape." She pulled out a big wad of matted hair. "I found this HUGE stash of Greek beards…"

At the far end, in his palatial seat, a shocked Hadrian stood up and raised his hand.

The crowd hushed.

"Zebra! You have fought gallantly today – as you did those many weeks ago when first we met. You have surprised many with your heroism and valour. It therefore gives me great pleasure to offer you, on this, my birthday, the wooden sword – the Rudis – a symbol of your well-earned freedom!"

Julius waited for the chanting and cheering to die down, then turned to the Emperor. "Hadrian, I thank you for your prize. But I cannot accept it."

Everyone gasped. Even Hadrian took a step back in shock.

"Not while my friends still fight for their *own* freedom," Julius continued. "Then, and only then – when the last one of us is free – will I take this honour from you!"

After a stunned silence, the crowd erupted once more into a chant of "ZEBRA! ZEBRA! ZEBRA!"

Hadrian spoke. "Zebra, you are either very wise or very foolish. Only time will tell." And with that, he disappeared to his palace, with the name ZEBRA ringing in his ears.

❦ EPILOGUE ❦

Six hundred miles away, just off the north coast of Africa, a rotting, ramshackle old arena – a quarter of the size of the mighty Colosseum – creaked in the blustery sea wind.

Only a few spectators had turned up to watch the second-rate gladiators, since all the best ones were in Rome for Hadrian's birthday bash. But at least some of the locals were still up for a good tussle, and Crixus – a hefty lump of a man – was always worth the entry fee.

There he stood now, in the middle of the sandpit, waiting for his opponent.

Crixus gripped his heavily spiked mace and watched in amazement as a very odd figure entered.

It looks like a horse, he thought. *A strange, stripy horse.*

"'Ere! What's all this nonsense?" he blurted. "I ain't fighting no horse!"

The stripy horse threw back his cloak and drew his sword, which glinted in the sun. "Not a horse," he said. "A zebra."

TO BE CONTINUED...

ROMAN NUMERALS

ROMAN NUMERALS

WAIT! We're not finished! There are two basic things you need to know to be able to count Roman numerals!

Oh?

1: YOU WILL NEVER FIND MORE THAN THREE ROMAN NUMERALS IN A ROW. 3 is written as III, but 4 is not IIII.

But hold on, how do you write 4 then?

My brain hurts!

2: WHEN A SMALLER NUMERAL COMES BEFORE A LARGER NUMERAL, TAKE AWAY THE VALUE OF THE SMALLER NUMERAL FROM THE BIGGER ONE TO WORK OUT THE NUMBER.

So 9 is IX?

Yes! You can remember it like this: 1 before 10 is 9.

To summarise: Always read Roman numerals from left to right, adding up as you go along. If a larger numeral comes before a smaller or equal numeral, add them together. But if a smaller numeral comes before a larger numeral, take away the value of the smaller numeral from the bigger one before moving on to the next letter in the row.

If there is a next letter, of course!

Here's some to help you along!

1	I	6	VI	11	XI	20	XX	70	LXX
2	II	7	VII	12	XII	30	XXX	80	LXXX
3	III	8	VIII	13	XIII	40	XL	90	XC
4	IV	9	IX	14	XIV	50	L	100	C
5	V	10	X	15	XV	60	LX	200	CC

AD GREGATIM: A large group fight normally saved for special occasions. Gladiators would re-enact mythological or historical battles; sometimes even staging naval battles with actual ships floating in amphitheatres filled with water!

AD INFINITUM: Latin phrase for something that goes 'on and on forever' (much like the waffling of a warthog).

AMPHITHEATRE: An ancient, open-air, oval-shaped stadium where the entertainment was less jolly and sporty, and more bloody and violent. Here gladiators would fight to the death, either against other gladiators or savage wild animals. The crowd loved it – the more blood the better! Tickets were free and some amphitheatres could seat up to 50,000 people; so you could easily have a lovely day out for the entire family.

AQUEDUCT: The Romans were actually very clean people and would have fresh water piped directly to their houses or local baths, sometimes from quite far-off distances. Complex engineering meant that the water delivered was so clean, even Julius would drink it.

BARRACKS: The name given to the gladiators' living quarters. Those who trained at the Ludus Magnus had rooms (some of which still survive today) which were very tiny; so any rock collections probably had to be kept to a minimum.

BATTLE OF ALESIA: A very important battle for the Roman General, Julius Caesar, which took place in 52BC. When he finally defeated the pesky Gauls, Julius strengthened his power in Rome, eventually becoming Dictator six years later.

CENTURION: A soldier of the Roman army who commanded 80 men (centuria) or more. Centurions wore big feathery or hairy crests on their helmets to make them stand taller than anyone else. A centurion's stick was his badge of rank in the army, but he was probably just as likely to hit you with it.

CHARIOT: A two-wheeled cart pulled by two (sometimes four) horses. They were used for zipping around in battles and had existed for thousands of years before the Romans adopted them for racing and ceremonies. In fact, Romans didn't just have horses to pull chariots; they used dogs, tigers, ostriches and even zebras, too!

CHARIOT RACING: Teams of chariots would race around the circuit of the Circus Maximus seven times in what was a deadly, but spectacular, sport. The citizens of Rome got very passionate about their four teams – Red, Green, Blue and White. Rivalries were so fierce, riots would start during races!

CIRCUS MAXIMUS: A spectacularly huge stadium, mainly used for chariot racing, seating up to 250,000 spectators; a quarter of Rome's population. The only way you'd find your friend among that lot was if they had a really long neck (or a massive moustache).

COLOSSEUM: The largest amphitheatre of the Roman Empire, the Colosseum sat in the centre of Rome itself and could hold up to 80,000 spectators. Here you would watch spectacles such as venatio, sea battles and, most important of all, gladiators! Built of concrete and stone, it was such a marvel of Roman engineering that it's still standing today!

COLOSSUS: The Colossus of Rhodes, standing at thirty metres tall, started a fashion in the ancient world for huge bronze statues depicting gods or emperors. The colossus at the centre of Rome stood next to the Flavian Amphitheatre, giving it the nickname by which we all know it today: the Colosseum!

EMPEROR HADRIAN: He ruled the Roman Empire between 117AD and 138AD, but rarely spent time in Rome! Hadrian much preferred to travel around the Empire making sure everything was in order. On a trip to the British Isles he famously built a very long wall – Hadrian's Wall – to keep out the Picts (a tribe living in northern Scotland) from England.

FAMILIA GLADIATORIA: These were the people who ran the gladiator school. The man in charge, the lanista, did pretty much everything from recruiting new gladiators to arranging training and organizing all the fights. It was probably quite stressful, all told.

FORESTS OF GERMANIA: Even though the Romans easily beat the Gauls in the Gallic Wars, they never had anywhere near the same success in Germania. In 9AD they lost a battle very badly in Teutoburg Forest, so the only way a Roman would get into the woods was from a swift kick up the bottom.

GAUL: This is what the Romans called the area now known as France, Belgium and Holland. Big hairy moustaches are still popular in the region to this day.

GERMANIA: This is roughly (sort of) where Germany is now (give or take large parts of other countries). They're also still pretty keen on moustaches.

GLADIATOR: Made up of slaves, criminals and any idiot who wanted in on the action, gladiators fought (usually to the death) against other gladiators or wild animals in the arenas of the Roman Empire.

GLADIATOR'S OATH: After reciting the Sacramentum Gladiatorium – "uri, vinciri, verberari, ferroque necari," which is Latin for "I will endure to be burned, to be bound, to be beaten, and to be killed by the sword" – you were sworn to the services of the gladiator school, with little chance of freedom.

GLADIUS: The sword of choice for the Roman army and the very same sword that gave us the name gladiator. Short and light, it was perfect for poking your enemy.

HISPANIA: The name the Romans gave to the Iberian Peninsula, which today consists of Spain, Portugal, Andorra and Gibraltar. The Hispanics also had moustaches, but less bushy ones.

IMPERIAL BOX: This is where the Emperor sat to watch all spectacles in the Colosseum. The box was elevated high up on a podium and adorned with flowing silk canopies and gold ornaments. You couldn't miss it, really.

JUPITER: One of the favourite Roman gods: the god of thunderbolts. You would usually call out to him when you stubbed your toe, or sat on a pin or something.

LANISTA: The boss of the gladiator school. He had lots to do around the place, so it was best not to ask him about a chafing subligaria.

LEPTIS MAGNA: A North African port, once part of Carthage, which was swallowed up by the Roman Empire after the 3rd Punic War of 146BC. Nowadays, the city is one of the most beautifully preserved Roman ruins.

LUDUS MAGNUS: Rome's biggest and best gladiator school. Built between 81 and 96AD, it sat right next to the Colosseum itself, with a tunnel linking the two.

PALUS: A big wooden pole stuck into the ground and used for sword training in the Roman army. The poles were supposed to represent your enemy, which would have been even more useful if the enemy were trees.

POENA CULLEI: A bizarre punishment where the condemned were sewn up in a leather bag with a snake, a dog, a cockerel and a monkey, then chucked into a river to drown. No doubt Jupiter probably got a few name calls along the way, too.

PORTUS AUGUSTI: The main port into which wild animals arrived from Africa. The unhappy cargo was then taken either via canal or via road direct to the city of Rome.

GARY'S GLOSSARY

QUAESTOR: The chap who sorted out the money for games in the Colosseum. He paid very well for zebras. But for warthogs … not so much.

RETIARIUS: A gladiator who fought with a net and a trident, a bit like a fisherman (a really horrible fisherman who would happily kill you just for the fun of it).

ROMAN ROADS: Romans liked their roads straight; it made it quicker to get from one place to another. Many of their roads still survive today. So if you're travelling on a straight road, it's most likely an old Roman road. Because it's straight.

RUDIS: If you were fortunate to win your freedom as a gladiator, you would also win the much sought after Rudis – a small wooden sword. A simple ornament that would brighten up any gladiator's mantlepiece.

SCISSOR: A fearsome gladiator who fought with blades and scythes

SESTERTII: A Roman coin. In Roman times, bread cost around 1/2 a sestertii and a donkey cost around 500 sestertii. Who knows how many thousand sestertii a zebra cost?

SUBLIGARIA: A loin cloth (a bit like a big nappy) which was most often worn by soldiers and gladiators. Chafing was always a danger!

SUMMA RUDIS: The referee during a gladiator fight. He wouldn't tolerate cheating. Well, not for less than 1,000 sestertii anyway.

SUPERSTITION: The Romans saw good or bad luck in everything: the shape of a cloud, the bark of a dog, wearing the wrong sandals on a weekend… Fortunately, in these modern times, being a Gemini, I don't believe in any of that nonsense.

TRIDENT: A three-pronged spear used by a retiarius.

VENATIO: Before the main gladiatorial fights, Romans were treated to the spectacle of thousands of wild animals – shipped in from around the Empire – hunted and killed by venators for blood-thirsty entertainment. They would even decorate the arena with trees so it looked like a real forest!

VENATORES: These were specialist gladiators who hunted wild animals in forests constructed in the arena for spectacles. The venatores were also on hand to train certain animals to do circus tricks, including monkey juggling.

VERNAL EQUINOX: This is when day and night is of equal length. A lucky day, if you've got the right pants on.

Gary Northfield has been writing and drawing comics since 2002. He is most famous for Derek the Sheep, a comic strip that appeared in *The Beano*. A collection of Derek the Sheep stories were published by Bloomsbury Children's Books. Gary has also created comics for *National Geographic Kids* magazine, *The Phoenix*, *The Dandy*, *The DFC*, *Horrible Histories* magazine, *Horrible Science* magazine and *The Magical World of Roald Dahl*. Most recently Gary published *The Terrible Tales of the Teenytinysaurs!* with Walker Books and *Gary's Garden* with David Fickling Books. One of Gary's favourite subjects is animals and their jolly lives, and he often wonders what they think about the world in which they live. Find Gary online at www.garynorthfield.com and on Twitter and Instagram as @gnorthfield.